# VISIONS

# VISIONS

## Metaphorical Mysteries

### STEVEN JENNEX

authorHOUSE®

AuthorHouse™
1663 Liberty Drive
Bloomington, IN 47403
www.authorhouse.com
Phone: 1-800-839-8640

© 2011 by Steven Jennex. All rights reserved.

No part of this book may be reproduced, stored in a retrieval system, or transmitted by any means without the written permission of the author.

First published by AuthorHouse    08/04/2011

ISBN: 978-1-4634-2377-3 (sc)
ISBN: 978-1-4634-2376-6 (ebk)

Library of Congress Control Number: 2011910250

Printed in the United States of America

Any people depicted in stock imagery provided by Thinkstock are models, and such images are being used for illustrative purposes only.
Certain stock imagery © Thinkstock.

This book is printed on acid-free paper.

Because of the dynamic nature of the Internet, any web addresses or links contained in this book may have changed since publication and may no longer be valid. The views expressed in this work are solely those of the author and do not necessarily reflect the views of the publisher, and the publisher hereby disclaims any responsibility for them.

# INFECTIOUS

### BY STEVE JENNEX

## The Curse.

Who would have thought a little computer programming could have come to this?

Even more unbelievable is the fact I'm not at all knowledgeable concerning the computer world, other than face book chat and internet surfing. Hence the reason I find it difficult to believe that my life has changed so drastically in such little time. Before I get ahead of myself, I should give an introduction. My name is Ben, Ben Wilson. I came from a farm property that I had lived on with my parents and my brother Danny. You know with all that has happened, I can't be sure anymore what city we lived on the outskirts of. Perhaps I've deliberately blocked the memory as to dissuade myself from recalling how this all began. To be honest, I couldn't tell you even now where I am or how I arrived here. A symptom of an undiagnosed disease, though I can't forget the details that brought me to write this. I only know I've been in this place several days, avoiding anyone and everyone. Behind the computer I sit searching for the solution, a cure to this nightmare. The occupants of this two-storey home either abandoned the place in search of safety or fell prey to the illness. They won't return, of this I'm certain. When I exhaust all recourses here such as food, clean clothes and electric power, only then will I venture out to another dwelling. Until then there is no need to put myself at risk. But here I am getting ahead of myself again. I will start at the beginning and fill you in from there.

Let's see, perhaps it is best I begin with Danny. A pain in the ass he was, with his need to do things his own way. I can't blame him though. It wasn't his fault he was born mentally slower than most. Mom blamed his condition on a fever she had while he was still in her womb and up until I saw her last, she still clung to that belief. The doctor's fault she claimed, for prescribing the wrong antibiotics. Yes he was a pain, yet we spent nearly every day together as we grew up. Someone had to protect him from the big bad world and I took it upon myself to do so. That's what big brothers are for after all, and the reason I became so eager when I believed I found a cure for his mental hindrance. It was less than a year ago. He was fourteen. I remember well, as we celebrated his birthday a week before I discovered the so-called miracle. I was busy downloading music and ignoring the unremitting doorbell chimes previous to him entering my bedroom. "Ben, Ben I need to talk to you Ben. This box came in the mail for you. See, it has your name on it. That's your name right there. Open it Ben, come on." "Alright, alright. How many times do you have to pester me today?" Okay, I could've been more pleasant, but if it were you being nagged in a similar manner on a constant basis, your patience would run short too. I'll never forget that ear to ear grin as he passed me the seemingly harmless package. "What is it Ben? Open it, I want to see." "Alright, slow down for Pete's sake. I can only do one thing at a time." I turned from the monitor and took the box from him. It was five to six inches cubed. My street name and house number was printed neatly by hand along with my first name, but no return address was given. Boxing tape held closed the bottom and top, whichever was which. I assumed the address was printed on the top. I used a pair of scissors I kept on my computer desk to neatly slice the tape at the seams, as to not damage the contents. I found it odd to observe no postage stamps and chose absolute diligence while prying open the flaps. Danny leaned in for a closer look as I peered inside. I knew by the weight not to expect much. Amongst Styrofoam peanuts I could see only a small silver rod which resembled the arm on a pair of glasses. "Stand back a bit." I told my brother as I knelt to dump the contents. He shuffled back and knelt with me. He said nothing which was unusual for his curious nature, as I poured out not only the Styrofoam, but what appeared to be headphones. A compact disc case fell out next and I scooped it up. "It's music, isn't it?" I dismissed Danny's inquiry and read a short message printed in the same ink and style as my name and address. 'To improve cognitive abilities and enhance your mental health, please read insert.' Danny picked up the headset and toyed with it while I took the opportunity to remove and unfold the insert. A set of instructions revealed the headset to be ocular with microscopic lenses that faced the pupil. They revealed digital information directly from the computer to the mind. The disc held the self-improving messages, or so the directions claimed. It was simple enough to use. Load the disc and plug the headset into the speaker outputs as though listening to music. There were no warnings or caution labels to be mindful of, just a company label. Occuchip Industry. Odd how a company such as this would send a free sample of their latest breakthrough. I should've been suspicious then, but like my brother, I was curious. After all, what could a little technology do? At worst cause a seizure, but I was prepared to watch for any adverse effects. If any arose I would simply throw away the defective product after breaking it to pieces. Still, with no warning labels the company must have deemed its product safe, which was all the encouragement I needed. Danny had the headset on, facing the wrong way. I popped the disc from the case and yanked it off his head. The wire which was previously wrapped with a twist tie, dangled to the floor. Danny reached for it but I pulled it away. "That wasn't nice, Ben. I was playing with that you know. You should ask before you take it." "Look bro," I said coolly, "I didn't see your name on it, did you?" He shook his head. "Good, now wait until I get it working and I'll let you try it, fair enough?" He nodded and stood as I took my place behind the desk. In no time I had the disc loaded and headset plugged in and placed correctly on my scalp. There was no instruction on the monitor, only a 'welcome to Occuchip. Press enter' greeting. Feeling somewhat hesitant, I positioned my finger over the 'enter' key, closed my eyes and pressed down. When I opened them, tiny white lights were shining at me through the optical lenses. They remained on for but a moment. When they went out I expected a flash of genius or a flood of universal oneness, but I was at the time, slightly disappointed. "Can you hear music? Can I try?" Danny twirled the twist tie around his finger and moved closer. I didn't know how to relay my lack of satisfaction other than to move out of the way and allow him to see for himself. "Here you go. Give it a try. Maybe something will happen for you." Those words make me cringe now as I recall the fascination he found with this new program. To this day, I have no idea what he had seen that I couldn't. I can still hear him list off the hallucinations that kept him at my desk every spare moment for five straight days. "The lights are all colors, Ben. Ben, did you see them? They are so pretty, like the paintings I made for mom." He referred to the water colors that mixed together like the designs on the tie-dye tee shirt. Once a month, mom would tack a fresh one on the fridge with magnets when he brought them home from school. Though clumsily created, they were still amusing enough to draw my attention and I found myself on more than one occasion, staring mindlessly into them. The twirling illustrations held me in a hypnotic state, which made me question who really held the intellect in the family. By the end of the fifth day I insisted to Danny, mom and dad that I need my space and he should stay out of my room for a while. Against his normal pattern of behavior, he simply smiled and agreed. That sent chills up my spine and I began to mentally note any changes in his conduct. For the first couple of weeks he was the same kid, though he spoke less and from time to time, talked to himself when he thought no one was listening. He also helped with chores which he usually weaseled out of. It wasn't until the third week when we were out on a bike ride that a noticeable and quite unexpected attitude change developed. We were further from home then we were permitted and found ourselves on foreign back roads. We had a few dollars each which was for a soda pop at the corner store. It was somewhere in the immediate area. We couldn't have been more than a few blocks away when Danny pulled off to the gravel shoulder to examine the street signs. Neither of us recognized the intersection. "Where are we, Ben? Are we lost?" I didn't know what to say as I stared over the stop sign. James and Logan were two streets rarely traveled by us and a half hour ride further than either of us had been. "No." I answered, hoping he wouldn't catch the hint of stress in my voice. He didn't. Instead he casually and confidently said, "The store we're looking for is two blocks away. We'll turn here and find it on the left." He pointed right up Logan drive. I was about to ask how he knew, but thought I could humor him by allowing him the lead. If the store wasn't there, we would simply ride back home the way we came. We may be let down, but no one would be to blame. Danny was used to being wrong most times anyway. So along the cracked, rough concrete we rode with the warm sun now in our faces. A subtle breeze wisped through my hair and I focused on the long dry grass waving gently at the edge of the road. After a moment an old faded green pick-up drove by and pulled off into a driveway about a block up. "The store is there." Danny said with an unsettling grin. "To the left where the truck is." Sure enough as we rode further, I picked out the sign on the face of the wood sided building. Curious George's market looked more like a mercantile from the western days than a traditional corner market, with its cracked and peeling whitewash finish. "Well I'm impressed. How did you know?" He said nothing as he dismounted his bike, but shot me a self satisfied smirk instead. We leaned our bikes against the wall beside the door and entered the store. Danny went to the service counter right away while I browsed the candy isle. Considering how isolated this place was, there were more customers than expected. Danny had to wait for a middle-aged woman who took her time deciding on what brand of cigarettes to take home to her husband. I noticed he was a touch irate and shuffled his feet nervously. I abandoned my window shopping and on my way to him, nearly bumped into the man driving the pick-up. He was courteous and even apologized for my error. The woman paid for her items and squeezed by on the way to the door. I can't forget the sweet waft of lavender perfume as she passed, nor the shy, nervous grin as she excused herself before pushing through the exit. It haunts me to know it was the last time anyone would see her smile. The pop was in a cooler behind the counter and Danny was having a tough time deciding what flavor to choose. He placed his money on the counter and eagerly scanned the bottles through the glass door. "Tough choice huh?" The cashier who I believed to be old George asked. Danny didn't respond with anything more than an anxious stare, so George chose grape crush for him. It was enough to settle him. He didn't like having to make decisions and George must've sensed any pop would have been satisfactory. I stood beside my brother and bought an orange soda. Outside the woman adjusted the radio dial and started the engine. When she saw Danny she placed her hands on the wheel and kept her eye on him. He stared back. To this day I don't know what chemistry they shared, but I caught the same brief twinkle of light in both their eyes. I now believe it to be a symptom of the computer program and the first of many glitches given by Occuchips brilliant device. I say brilliant with notable sarcasm. Two days later that same woman appeared as a top news story. She had evidently gone straight home after shopping and slaughtered her husband and two young children with a butcher knife before slashing her own throat. How can I forget her cold dead stare prior to driving off?

After the news story, I jogged to my bedroom and removed the disc from the hard drive. I knew then in some way it bore responsibility for the death of that family. I didn't wish to chance the same results with mine and snapped it in two before throwing it in the waste basket. I yanked the headset out and was about to toss it as well, but I remembered my science teacher Mr. Morris, and chose to have him examine it.

Danny and I didn't chum around like we used to once the disc and headset were no longer available. He acted as though he held some grudge because I removed his addiction. He chose to spend his time in solace and either stayed in his room or at the school playground when he wasn't in class. That's how I remember him; a lonely, sad teenager. It's been some time from the last visit we had. He didn't speak at all then and probably hasn't since. How distant he looked from behind the plexiglass partition. I wondered if he was still alive, or if the virus finally caught up with him like most everyone else. Perhaps time would tell.

Back to Mr. Morris. The day I handed him the headset, he looked at me like I had two heads. "What am I to do with this?" He asked before I could explain. My answer was simple enough. Examine it, of course. I didn't go into great detail, but explained how my brother was getting headaches after using it. Yeah, I know, not exactly honest, but what else could I say? I didn't want to scare him. If he knew what I knew he'd have questioned my sanity. Still I was sure there was no danger as the disc had been destroyed. "Come back the day after tomorrow. I'll give you my results then." Fair enough I thought on my way out the door.

Mr. Morris didn't return to school the next day nor the day after, which prompted me to look up his address and pay him a visit. So I skipped class that Friday morning and tracked down his house. Thank goodness he lived three blocks past the school, and not closer to the city core. I rode my bike up the driveway, lay it by the walkway and strolled to the front door. While I awaited an answer to my knock, I glanced around the neighborhood. Nothing out of the ordinary, though it was unusually quiet. Mr. Morris' car was not in the car port so I assumed from the lack of response he wasn't home. I was becoming concerned that with his sudden absence something may have happened. My thoughts went directly to my mystery gift as the culprit, considering how it changed Danny. Some doubt remained as he didn't have the disc, but still . . . I turned the door knob. I don't know what I was thinking. I knew I wanted the headset back and to snoop for clues, but did that constitute break and enter? The door was unlocked and I gave the area a final glance before slipping inside.

The place was a disaster. There were papers strewn everywhere and broken glass from the picture frames which left their silhouettes on the walls, littered the floor. I crept past the overturned couch and into the kitchen. A metallic scent filled the room. The cluttered counter was the only mess, along with what I took to be dried hamburger blood splashed on its surface. A few flies buzzed over the sink and I peered inside. More blood, much more than from a hamburger package. Maybe he cut himself on the fillet knife that lay in the crusty goo, thus explaining his absence. He could be in the hospital, but for two days? Not likely. An uneasy feeling swept through my body and suddenly all I wanted was to find the headset and leave. Quickly I scurried about the living area, kicking away broken frames and exploring the entertainment center before heading down the hall toward the bedroom. That's when I heard a thump similar to a cupboard door dropping shut. It came from the bathroom. Cautiously I crept there, following a blood trail I hadn't noticed before. I leaned into the doorway and cocked my ear. The trail led to the bathtub. I wanted to follow it, but my pounding heart told me I'd better find what caused the noise. I didn't need to wait long because one of the cupboards below the counter popped open, throwing my adrenaline to overdrive. Then immediately, something leapt out and stood staring in my direction. My fears settled and I knelt to coax over the black fir ball Mr. Morris called Charcoal. "To bad you can't speak." I cooed as the cat rubbed its face against my outstretched hand. "I'm sure you'd have quite the story to tell." I guess he or she had no desire for chit chat because it bolted toward the living room and disappeared into the kitchen. 'Crazy animal,' I thought as my attention returned to the blood. Mr. Morris had mentioned his cat on a few occasions. In fact, he spoke of both of them, usually while describing dexterity and balance as all things shared in nature. The other was an orange tabby he referred to as Cat. Not very creative for a teacher, but to the point. I half expected it to jump out as Charcoal had. I neared the tub. The opaque shower curtain was closed and ruby smears and hand prints turned some of the white to dirty pink.

I shouldn't have thrown up in the sink, thus leaving my D.N.A. in the house but I suppose it was better than upchucking on the crime scene. You may be guessing by now that I found Cat, gutted and hanging by the neck via a yellow chord. The poor think had been disemboweled and its paws lay in congealing blood below. Asphyxiation was likely the cause of death. So there I was, staring into an imbrued bathtub and wondering why I'd been so careless. Mr. Morris was paying for my ignorance and possibly anyone who crossed his path. I wondered what he found out about the headset as I completed my search of the house. I also wanted to know what he did with it. If he'd taken it with him, I'd never see it again. As it was that's exactly what happened.

I told nobody of what I'd discovered and I honestly don't think anyone cared. I returned to my swiftly changing life and Mr. Morris vanished into the wind. Kind of him to tell his superior he wouldn't be returning to work. I believe the principal told our class he was on a permanent vacation. I bet the conversation was more to the point of 'take this job and shove it.' Likely with a few choice words to go with it. Either way we now had a new teacher, Miss Mackey. Much easier on the eyes she was, but lacking Morris' witty style.

# The Search

Shortly after, Danny was committed to the hospital for a psyche exam. I said my goodbyes to mom and dad and headed off on my own. I didn't know what kind of mission I thought I was on, nor did they. I left them with the impression I was staying with a friend. Dishonest I know, but it kept their queries to a minimum. I kept telling myself I needed to track down Occuchip industries and find out their motives for mailing me the curse. They must've wanted to stay anonymous, as I could find no trace of them whatsoever. Not on an internet listing, not in the phone book. I went so far as to ask a private investigator to help my search. He agreed that if he was unable to find the company, I would not be charged. True to his word, I was not flipped a bill and Occuchip remained underground. For the next month or so I lived in any shelter that would have me. Being younger than nineteen I had to rely on the odd church, which would carry me a few days at a time. I suppose they'd seen homeless youth before, for they weren't quick to pry into my personal life. Other times I slept in alleys, under an overpass or two and even broke into an unfinished apartment suite. I traveled from my home town to other cities and small towns along route as I aimlessly headed any direction my weary mind would guide me. What possessed me not to return home? I'd have to say the recent bad memories. Periodically I would daydream of Mr. Morris and what he could be doing. His butchered feline burned in my thoughts up until the day my worst fears came true. I was walking through a mall in some quaint little village in the middle of nowhere, when I was distracted by a television in a home electronics store. I hadn't so much as read a newspaper, let alone watched a news program. As though meant to be, I turned the volume on the display model. Wouldn't you know it; there was Mr. Morris' photo. From the partial story I absorbed, he had been cornered by police and shot when he dragged a knife across the throat of his hostage. She survived, but the twelve other hitchhikers, both male and female, had been brutally tortured before their slow execution. So that's where he'd been. Good-bye Mr. Morris, nice to have known you. I felt ill the rest of the day and chose to sleep in an alley that night. I found a cardboard bin as my bed. There were several collapsed boxes lining the bottom and because it was nearly empty, I knew I wouldn't be dumped into a compactor by morning. The repulsive odor of urine and rotten food contaminated my nostrils and I wondered why I didn't go to the shelter instead. Once again I was following my instincts and as always the reason was made clear before dawn. It wasn't the hoots and hollers from the bar patrons as they staggered down the streets which woke me, nor the lighter clicks from the drug users that took refuge in the doorways. It was a whisper above the others coming from behind my dumpster that drove me from my dreams into my living nightmare. Not the volume or pitch, but what the guy I came to know as crazy Larry, was saying. Between the curses and mumbles came a three syllable word that piqued my interest and sent shivers up and down my spine. Occuchip. Slowly I raised my head and peered over the rim, directly into the brightest green eyes I've ever seen. In the dim glow of security lights, crazy Larry stared back like a deer caught in headlights. "Who are you?" He promptly asked. "What do you want?" "I could ask the same as you." I cooed. "After all, you woke **me**. I heard you mention a familiar name." "I got no idea what you're babblin' about." He returned as he nervously switched his stance. "You oughtta mind your own business." He turned his back to me and carried on digging through his frayed blue backpack. I took the opportunity to climb from the bin and waited for him to turn around. When he did, he frowned. With more annoyance than hostility, he asked, "You still here? Is there somethin' you want? I don't have much, the clothes on my back, and if I'm lucky my sanity." He picked his pack up by one strap. The zipper was open and I caught a glimpse of something familiar. The reason I'd taken up the quest in the first place. He caught the shock on my face and hurriedly tugged the zipper. "Where'd you get those?" I pointed to the pack before he could close it. He knew right away I was referring to the computer headset. "You don't want them, nothin' to do with 'em. Trouble they are. Nothin' but trouble. Now mind yourself and get on your way. I got things to do." With the zipper closed, he slung the pack over his shoulders. "Let me guess," I curtly added, "A gift from Occuchip." At the mention of the corporation he waved his hands in my face and shushed me. "Are you crazy? Don't mention that name so loud. You'll end up . . ." "What?" I interrupted, "homeless?" "Yeah," he agreed. His mannerisms reflected an understanding we both shared. I must've broken through his barriers. "Or dead. My name's Larry. People call me crazy Larry, so have your pick of either one. Better they think your nuts anyhow." He toned down to a whisper. "Keeps big brother off your back, know what I mean?" Of course he meant the cops, but I know he was thinking of the thugs from Occuchip. Though I hadn't met up with any, I'm certain they existed. Why else would they be so secretive? To protect their mob connections or whatever group funded them, of course. "You've used the headset, haven't you?" Larry lowered his eyes and motioned for me to sit. I lay my back against the dumpster and we sat abreast. I expected him to smell as acrid as our surroundings and was pleasantly surprised at the scent of skin bracer and shampoo. He began his story by answering my inquiry. "Yeah, several times. I figured it would clear my mind and make me wiser like the ad promised. Instead, I found myself wandering wherever my thoughts would take me, like being dragged by an invisible leash. I still don't know where I'm goin' or what I'm searchin' for, but I can't seem to stop myself." I assured him I understood completely before he described the side effects his family suffered through. "My dad was the second to try it out, followed by my sister. She didn't last long. Started babbling about voices in her head before the hallucinations began. They lasted just over a week before she hung herself in the tree in our back yard. That's when mom and dad separated. She left without a word to me. Still one thing that bothers me is the flash of light in her eye before she told dad she'd rather kill'em than look at him. Guess she blamed him for Sally's death. Next thing I know I'm on the run. Haven't heard from dad since. You know," he said with a chuckle, "I'm surprised I remember so much. Seems as though everything I've done since I left home has been a blur. I feel like I'm walkin' in a daydream. Still don't know what city I'm in." "Know what you mean." I intervened. "I just keep wandering, searching for anything Occuchip related. And now I've found you, so where do we go from here?" In my mind, I hoped he wouldn't want to hang around with me too long. This was my solitary journey and I wished to share information and nothing more. "I wanna dissect this contraption and find out how it works. I wanna study the disc closer too." The disc! He had one. Would he be willing to part with it? My mind began to race at that point and I found myself mentally breaking down scenarios on how to take it from him. Hopefully, it wouldn't come down to stealing. I chose to change the subject. "Did you have any other side effects like violent thoughts?" "No, none at all, you?" I explained of Danny's behavior changes, how his confidence significantly boosted but didn't result in violence. I mentioned the woman who locked eyes with him and the flickering glow in their pupils before she murdered her family. The same flash he'd witnessed in his mother. I told him of Mr. Morris and his tantrum that destroyed his furniture and cat before he embarked on a killing spree. "Memory loss too. Town and street names mostly, since leaving home to come to this." I motioned an empty hand to our surroundings. "We're gonna have to go to the library to use their computer. How about first thing tomorrow?" I promptly agreed. "Good, best get some sleep. I'll take you there in the morning." He crawled behind the dumpster as I climbed back in bed. Pulling a cardboard sheet across my legs, I began to wonder if indeed we were being monitored somehow. I closed my eyes and fell into a fitful sleep.

There were two of them. I couldn't make out their faces but I could hear them talking about me as they hovered around the gurney I lay on. "He's not showing any signs of infection." One of the shadows said. A dim grey luminescence enveloped the background. There was a strong chemical smell in the air and I could feel tubes running into my arms. My bare chest had sticky pads adhered over my ribcage. I was in a laboratory of sorts. "Keep monitoring him for a few more days. If he shows no signs by then, place him with the others." In a flash I was being escorted down a dreary hallway toward the sound of troubled souls. My two guides stood me before a heavy metal door with a tray slot near the bottom. I knew I was about to be tossed into a cell I'd never leave alive. One guard unlocked the door. Before I could be shoved inside, the tray door banged open and a bony hand jutted out and grabbed my leg . . . "Wake up, we've gotta make the meal line before they close." I jerked from the nightmare. Larry had me by the ankle and was shaking me. He abruptly stopped when I jolted up. He pulled back as I stretched, yawned and clambered from the bin. "What time is it?" I asked. "Don't know, don't care. All I know is it's meal time. We gotta hurry before we miss out." After a five minute walk, we arrived at a soup kitchen that fed the poor breakfast, lunch and dinner. There was a short wait in line before we grabbed our trays. Eggs, sausage and slightly charcoaled toast with premixed powdered milk was today's menu. "We got lucky." Larry said as he nudged me with his elbow. "Yesterday was cold cereal and the toast was rock hard. Someone's watchin' over us." My thoughts returned to my dream. Someone's watching alright, from inside our brains, and we let them in. "You gonna finish those?" Larry noticed me picking at the scrambled eggs. He pointed to the sausages. "No, help yourself." I wasn't hungry anyway. I was more concerned about what we'd find on the computer or who'd find us. I hoped Larry was a hacker. My basic knowledge wouldn't get us very far. I'd soon find out.

Within a half hour we took our post at the regional library computer. Larry had to use his card to grant us access. He informed me he forged a bogus name as to keep his anonymity, thus throwing off any info that could trace back to him. A wise idea considering the circumstance, even if the enemy was imagined. As he loaded the disc, I nervously glanced around to make sure no one paid us special interest. I didn't know what made me so uneasy. I'd been lit up since the nightmare and couldn't help but feel scrutinized. I had to convince myself my emotional expansion was due to Occuchips brain washing. Larry began by scanning the internet for any site related to our nemesis. After ten minutes of occult and occupational therapy sites, I had to use the men's room. I told Larry I'd be back shortly and left his side. When I returned a few minutes later, Larry was digging through his pack sack. On the screen were the words 'Occuchip insert headset' in small print, bottom right corner. The screen changed color like a kaleidoscope. Larry withdrew the headset. Quickly I moved to block any view of his actions. "Are you crazy?" I gruffly whispered. "You're gonna get us busted." You would've thought we were robbing a bank had you overheard how stressed my point was. Larry down played my nervousness. "Relax, I'm almost there. I've never been to this site before and I don't know if I could get back in. This is our only chance." I moved aside as he plugged the headset in and turned it on. I wish I could have seen through his eyes right then as he feverishly danced his fingers along the keyboard. "Wow," he exclaimed. "The info I'm retrieving is phenomenal. I could tell you all you need to know about Occuchip. Members, locations, I . . ." The clacking of the keyboard ceased with his sentence. His arms fell to his side and he stared into the screen. It took but a few seconds for him to regain his composure and he reached over to unplug the headset jack. At first I didn't believe anything to be different, other then accumulation of information. When he placed the headset and disc into the pack sack, I discovered how wrong I was. It wasn't when he pushed the contents down and pulled the zipper closed that I noted the change in his persona. No, the revelation came when he reached for something in his sock and turned his attention to me. The flash in his pupils was unmistakable and briefly I imagined how that poor family felt before they were butchered. The urge to run was great. After all, if one dainty woman could easily take down her adrenaline pumped husband, how much easier for Larry to plunge his switch blade into my chest. He kept the knife low and stepped forward as I raised my hands. I shuffled back a step or two and softly said, "You don't wanna do this. We're on the same side." "I have to," he calmly replied. "It's for the greater good." He showed no emotion. I would've been less troubled if he was angry. Anger can trip you up, cause you to make mistakes, and it was painfully obvious he wasn't about to let that happen. "We can discuss this." A commotion to my right took a portion of my focus off Larry. My eyes stayed on him as my hearing caught a partial sentence from a woman at the information desk. 'Knife' and 'police' were all I needed to hear. Crazy Larry who was living up to his name must have heard it to, for he lunged at me right then. He swung the blade at my throat and I jumped away. I heard it slice the air under my chin. A woman shrieked and two city security guards quickly rushed up behind me. "Drop it!" One demanded as he reached for the taser. I dodged between them and headed for the exit. Two armed cops nearly knocked me down as I reached the door. Curiously, I turned to check on Larry only to wish I hadn't. One of the security guards was on his knees and holding his stomach. Larry stood over him and plunged the knife through the back of his neck. With blood squirting in all directions, the other guard ran to a book shelf and hid. The cops didn't say a word. No warning, no commands. Instead they let their service weapons speak for them. Larry caught the first slug in the arm and the knife dropped. I couldn't bear witness any longer. I bolted out the door and toward the first alley I could find. Two more shots rang out and I winced as I pictured them tearing through his chest and head. As siren wails grew closer, I ducked into a doorway and held my ears as they screamed past. When they were beyond me, I ran until I could no longer breathe. Several blocks away, I collapsed behind the same dumpster where it all began. I wanted to cry and my body vibrated from shock. No tears came, only the contents of my stomach as I puked my lunch onto the concrete. When done, I pushed off the red brick wall and staggered to the dumpster. I dropped along side it and propped against the cold steel. My eyes were closed and hands to my face. The glint of light from Larry's lifeless stare haunted me. I had the feeling he had transferred something to my memory as Danny had when he stared at the woman outside the store. I had no psychotic thoughts so I somehow knew I hadn't been subjected to the infectious programming. Still, some needed information was planted, I was certain.

Two days later, I read about the incident in the local paper. I couldn't tell you the name of the paper, or I'd let you know what city I was in at the time. Details of that nature still evaporate before I can recall having them. Every home, every town is the same. A consistent flow as different yet familiar as the ever changing sky. Though I despise the memory glitch, I know deep down it has its purpose. Regardless, Larry had been killed by a bullet to the head after sustaining one in the chest. Exactly as I knew it happened. The police were searching for me to explain what conspired to cause him to go nuts. They apparently wanted to know how I 'provoked' him. Their words, though I knew someone high up understood the situation fully. Though it was not mentioned, his back pack was taken and no doubt searched. Occuchip must be run by powerful characters in order to maintain this cover up.

# SURVIVAL

I stayed in the shadows from then on and moved on to the next town. Survival meant more as each day my fear of being followed heightened. No one suspicious ever reared their head as though I was discarded as non-threatening. The thought gave little comfort as I slinked through people's garages and yards in search of food and shelter. My dreams no longer consisted of capture and probing as they had when Larry was alive. His death seemed to throw those fears out the window. I was off the Occuchip hit list, but that didn't end the horror. I can tell you as I type out this diary that it was just the beginning of a more terrifying reality. Read on and you'll know what I mean. I'll begin with the very creepy and unplanned trip to one of the local high schools. Why go to a public high school, is what you must be asking yourself. It didn't make much sense to me at first either as I read about the sudden boost of intelligence brought on by a computer game. I knew right away what the paper was referring to, which was more reason to question my sanity as I walked up the concrete steps to the main doors. Blame curiosity, I convinced myself as I made my way through the corridors to the computer lab. The school was small, consisting of less then two hundred students and was named after some large toothed mammal. Home of the otters, I'll call it, being I'm confused by the cascade of animal faces as I try to recall the one. Yes, otter will do fine. Now enough of falling off topic. I did find my way to the computer lab with no problem. Any students who passed by didn't care about my grubby appearance and simply grinned as though accepting me as one of their own. There was no shouting or shoving. No bullies picking on smaller students. No running in the halls or gossiping as teenage girls often do. This school was prim and proper, lacking nothing but a dress code. My guard was up immediately. At the lab I peered inside. There was no need to enter. I saw the source of their intellect from the door. Attached to every keyboard was an Occuchip headset. My heart began to pound and as if sensing my nervousness, the whole class turned my way. I don't have to tell you how quickly I left. The tread streaks burned in the linoleum were proof enough. Just teasing, though I nearly dislocated my shoulder slamming into the exit door. When off the property, I chanced a glimpse back. There were no students following, nobody at all but the elderly gent watching from the main entrance. I gathered he must be the principal. He said nothing and made no gestures my way, so I continued in a speed walk to the nearest street that would cover me from his view.

An hour later I stood at a shelf in the local food bank. This one doubled as a thrift shop and was run by a Christian organization. I grabbed a bag of donuts and was about to leave when a grey haired woman called to me. "Would you like something more substantial?" she asked. "We have a kitchen in the back. There is still soup and sandwiches left over from lunch." How could I resist such an offer after dining on dumpster scraps all week?

Of course I accepted. Cream of broccoli soup was today's dish. I sprinkled pepper on top and stirred it in as the woman named Emma brought me two egg sandwiches. She reminded me of my grandmother by the way she called me son. She asked if I needed any clothes as I slurped the soup off the spoon. I nodded and she left me to finish my meal. After two bowls and four sandwiches I was full and a little weary. Emma led me through the clothing department and allowed me two of each item. I didn't much feel like lugging around forty pounds of clothes, so I declined one pair of jeans and asked for a pack sack instead. She found a black one suitable for my needs and placed my clothes into it. I took it from her and set the donuts on top before zipping it closed. After thanking her, I started for the door. "Wait son." She hurried over with a business card. "If you need a place to sleep, come here around six tonight. We'll provide a meal and do your laundry." Again I thanked her and stuck the card in my back pocket. I wouldn't need it tonight. I was still leery of these folks so I'd keep to my routine. Just in case, I didn't stray far and set up camp behind a convenience store two blocks away. As I said, I was weary, and by five I was asleep under a clear sky with a pack for a pillow and cardboard for cover. I actually prayed that night, giving thanks for lack of rain and all the various necessities to make my life bearable.

When I awoke, it was dark and voices could be heard whispering nearby. I knew right away they were people my age, students from the local high school. "I know he's here somewhere." I heard a young woman say. "Aunt Emma said he went this way." "Why couldn't you get her to keep him there?" A gruff young man asked. "What am I supposed to do, have her chain him up? You know she's too good for that." He grumbled and said, "Never mind. Find him. We have to shut him up." You're wondering how I got out of it, aren't you? I didn't sneak away as you may think. To my own surprise I actually stood up and stepped out from behind the dumpster. There were five of them, two girls and three guys. At the sight of me the men stepped forward. "There you are," the blonde in the middle stopped short. His buddies stood beside him, arms crossed. I opened my mouth to speak but was denied. "What were you doing at our school, you a spy or something? You know what we do with spies?" He held his open hand to his side. The friend to his right pulled something from his jacket and handed it to him. A metallic glint reflected in the dim light. My chest tightened and I felt panicked. I nearly peed myself when he pointed the pistol at me and cocked the hammer. "I was checking it out." I said in a shaky voice. "I thought I might attend next semester." The kid gave me a curious smirk. My head began to spin and a cascade of recent experiences flooded my memory. Was this what was meant by your life flashing before your eyes? "Woah, did you see that?" Buddy to the left tapped blondie on the shoulder with the back of his fingers. The girls who were looking on with smug attitude stepped up. **"I** saw it." The one closest to pretty boy said. I hadn't noticed before, but she had red streaks in her ebony hair. She had it parted over her right eye, which gave her a look I could only describe as childish and punky, definitely my type. The way she sized me up gave me the impression she had some interest but wouldn't show it in view of her friends. "Saw what?" The other said. She had a more preppy facade with a hint of snob. "He's one of us," said blondie. "Where are you from?" I had no reply. Half the time I could barely recall my name. Strangely he answered for me as though reading my mind. "You don't know, do you? You've probably been wandering aimlessly for weeks." He lowered the gun. "Our school has no room for your kind. You know, rejected. Get outta here. Wander back home if you can find it. You'll be safer." "Wait a minute." I demanded. I stepped forward as he turned to leave. In defense he whirled around and stuck the barrel of the gun an inch from my nose. Ignoring his threat I spat. "What are you talking about? Rejected by who?" All five began to chuckle. He spread his arms and looked to his comrades. "By us of course. You didn't take. Why do you think you're wandering aimlessly? A dog without a home is all you are, but hey, look on the bright side. You're not even worth a bullet." In rapid succession, he squeezed the trigger twice. I flinched, expecting it to go off, but the hammer only clicked. "Consider yourself fortunate you've been marked or you'd be dead." "Marked?" I asked. "How?" He pointed to his eye. "It's all in here my friend. Do yourself a favor, leave town while you can." The five headed into the shadows, giggling and chatting amongst themselves. Chatting of how pathetic I was. Disheartened, I went back to my bed and pondered blondie's words. 'It's all in here, my friend.' All in the eyes, the windows to the soul. Marked he said, but how? Something in my eyes gave me away. I chose to sleep on it and curled up under the cardboard.

"Like a wandering dog. Not even worth a bullet." Blondie threw his head back in laughter and vanished into the dark. Two men approached. One wore a suit, the other a white overcoat. "He didn't take. Put him with the others." They led me down a narrow corridor to the familiar metal door. The food slot popped open as I glanced down and a bony hand held out a headset. "Not for you." The gravelly voice snorted. The headset disintegrated to dust. When it floated to the floor it became blood. I turned to the man in the suit. He turned me to face the man in white and held my hands behind me. I couldn't break free. The man in white held up a long syringe. His eyes went black and he brought it to my jugular . . . Something grabbed my shoulder and I jerked up. The person shaking me came into clarity. It was the pretty girl with red streaks. I wasn't sure if I was still dreaming so I tested myself by grabbing her hand. She was real alright. "Get up, we need to talk. Come with me." Disoriented, I stood. A wave of dizziness hit and I stumbled after her. Where she was taking me was any ones guess. "You better not be setting me up for a beating." "Don't be silly." She whispered, "And keep quiet." We headed the same direction I had come in. Not surprisingly we ended up at the thrift store. We rounded the building to the rear exit and she tapped three times on the door. In a moment an elderly woman opened it. It was Emma. "Hi, Auntie." She hustled us inside. "Clover, so good to see you." "Call me Cloey, you're embarrassing me." Her face reddened and she gave me a sheepish grin. "My name is Cloey, like Zoë." "You need not be ashamed." I reassured her. "Clover is a pretty name." With shy, childlike innocence, she turned to Emma and changed the subject. "This is . . . what's your name?" "Ben." I answered abruptly. Her flirtatious smile and humble mannerisms entranced me enough to forgive her unintended insult. "He's a reject." I rolled my eyes. "Alright, no need to be spiteful." Emma said as she led us to the kitchen where I had my last meal. "You know what I mean, Auntie. His program didn't take. For some reason he's not violent like the others. He's special." She gave me a pleasing smile and I melted. I think I was falling in love. "Does anyone know you're here?" "No, I don't believe so. Can you put him up tonight?" "Of course, there's plenty of room." "You said we need to talk." I pressed. "What do you need to know?" "I need to know what **you** know. Has anyone you know gone insane lately? Anyone you've been in contact with?" "Besides myself?" I jested. "Yeah, a couple. Why?" Emma stood. "I'm going to bed. Make yourselves at home. I'll see you in the morning." She headed for a staircase that most likely led to her suite. "She lives up there?" Clover nodded. "I need you to focus. Did their moods change while making eye contact with you?" I shook my head. "No, but a woman I met outside a store killed her whole family shortly after my brother stared at her." I spilled out my story as though I'd known her all my life. "He had this white flash in his pupils. It's as though he hypnotized her. I can't describe it any other way. My teacher also went loopy after using my headset. You know the kind you have in your computer lab? The ones from Occuchip." "Occuchip? Never heard of it. Ours were ordered in by our principal." "Believe me," I reassured, "they're from the same company." "So it appears Justin was right. You're one of a kind." "No, there was one other. His name was Larry. We were trying to track down Occuchip together. We used a library computer to find their location, but it went bad. Something happened to him when he used his headset. He attacked me and the cops killed him. I saw the same light in his eyes. Does that mean I'm gonna lose it like that woman? Am I infected?" "Only one way to tell." Cloey held my hand and squared off to me. Her tantalizing perfume wafted my way and I closed my eyes. "Open them," she demanded. "Wipe that grin off and stare into mine. If you see anything abnormal, tell me." I didn't want to risk her going crazy but I didn't want to disappoint her either. Reluctantly I stared into her beautiful blue irises. She stroked the back of my hand with her thumb. Whether she was flirting or putting me at ease was difficult to tell. Several seconds later she pushed away. "You seem to be normal. I didn't notice any change. Your pupil glow is calming, not at all harmful." Pupil glow? That was the first time I realized how strongly the headset affected me. I had no idea what blondie had meant by 'he's one of us.' The glow must have revealed itself when I became nervous. Apparently it was controlled by extreme emotion, which begged the question, which emotion was Cloey receiving? "I didn't see one in you. Is that bad?" "No, sometimes it's better. It shows I'm not affected by you. We're compactable because you can't be dangerous to me." "What about others? Why do they go crazy?" She motioned me to the table I had eaten at and we sat down. "My principal told us there was a virus in some of the software. It affects different people in different ways. Five students have been hauled away for erratic behavior. There's been no major violence here, but we've seen it on the news. The last so far was the worst. You probably heard about him. He killed twelve hitchhikers." "That would be Mr. Morris, my science teacher." I cut in. "Why would your school continue using the program if it can cause so much damage?" She brushed her hair to one side. I couldn't help but long to press my lips to hers. Her pink lipstick brought new depth to her beckoning pout. "Our school has a very high success rate. Some of our grade eight students are at a second year college level. I'm already doing first year university calculus. Not bad for a grade ten student." Perfect, she was my age. I couldn't get too excited though. After all, she had a home. I was no more than a dog wandering lonely city streets. I lowered my eyes in shame and wondered if anything would ever be the same. I had my doubts. She must have felt my pain, for she again took my hand. "I'm sorry it didn't work out for you. You're so nice. I can't imagine the hell you've been through." "It's not over yet." I mumbled before a hard yawn. My energy was drained and all I wanted was to crawl back to my corrugated room. "I should get going. I left my belongings behind the bin." "No," her seductive whisper blew over me like a gentle breeze. "You stay here. I'll grab your backpack and bring it to . . ." I don't know what came over me. She had to have been right about our compatibility. As we kissed I expected her to pull away and slap my face. Instead she placed her hand behind my head and stroked my hair. Our lips were together for no more than ten seconds, but it felt like a heavenly lifetime. My cares melted and my problems evaporated. I wish it could last forever. When she pulled away, she caressed my cheek. Before she could speak I uttered, "My belongings can wait." We held each other through the night as we cuddled on the floor between coat racks. It was nice to sleep with a sleeping bag, though I woke periodically from twisted dreams. I would fall back to my dream world only after gazing upon her innocence while she lay her head close to my shoulder. Her presence dissolved any concern for the future. Things were good again.

"Get up you two. The store opens in forty-five minutes. School starts in an hour and fifteen, Clover. I don't want you late for class." Cloey raised her head off my chest. "Thanks auntie M." She said as she strained to make eye contact. "Good morning." She pushed herself to her knees and brushed tangled hair strands aside. "Good morning to you." I replied. My stomach growled. "My aunt will make us a hot breakfast. I can smell it already. You up for pancakes and sausage?" "Am I ever. First I need the bathroom." "Against the far wall, right of the C.D's and books." In the mirror I studied my features. I had lost weight, at least five pounds since leaving home. More likely closer to ten. My cheeks were sunk in somewhat. My irises were brighter than usual, more green than brown. Mom used to say hazel eyes had a way of brightening or darkening depending on the mood. Before meeting Cloey they were likely dark brown. I must have been staring into them for at least a minute when a flood of disturbing images raced through my thoughts. I could see Cloey's class mates, the ones who confronted me. Blondie or Justin as she called him, was not happy. His penetrating frown was directed my way and I knew he would do Cloey harm because of me. His two pals held baseball bats and the snobby girl held the gun. Though they didn't move, I could feel their rage and the strike of the first swing as it collapsed my ribs. I had the painful forethought Cloey was next. The vision passed and for the first time I caught the white flash that had saved me last evening. I shook my head and gained my composure. I wouldn't let Cloey know what I'd seen. Perhaps we'd have been better off if I had.

After breakfast, Cloey walked me to my belongings. I was pleasantly surprised no one had rummaged through them. I was equally pleased she held my hand the few blocks. She kissed my cheek and hugged me prior to heading to school. I didn't set up a meeting place for after, so I chose to spend one more night at Emma's. Surely she would stop in after school. I had nothing important to do the rest of the day, so I took Emma up on her offer for a hot shower before lunch. Afterward she washed my clothes while I snacked on a couple of donuts. I clearly recall the less than pleasant odor as I handed them over and the sharp smell of body odor from under my pits as I stepped under the spray. Why Cloey hadn't mentioned her distaste was beyond me, so either she didn't notice or was being polite. It showed how much she cared. Yup, she was a keeper. When lunch was done I set my pack on a cot set out for me. I needed fresh air and headed off to explore this new town. Its center was five or so blocks from the high school. I traipsed through electronics shops and hobby stores to tease myself. I loved radio controlled devices, especially air planes and cars. Dad and mom bought me a Ferrari Testarossa from a store like Zellers or Wal-Mart a year ago. It lacked any real power and couldn't be driven over anything as rough as shag carpet. The cars in these stores were much higher quality and very expensive. Some were nitro fuel powered and could hit speeds of seventy kilometers per hour. Those were the toys I longed for. Good luck affording any now. I checked into a computer store as well, curious to find newly released video games. "What do you have for racing games that are compatible with I.B.M?" I asked the nerdy looking gentleman behind the counter. I wasn't going to buy one of course, nor steal it. I was window shopping to kill time, but if they had any sample games hooked up, I'd try a few. "Anything new will be against the far wall." He pointed me in the right direction and picked up a flyer. As he read on I caught him stealing a glance my way. I must've looked penniless. Before I reached the games a cardboard display caught my eye. It had the company name printed below a picture of the merchandise. It was the Occuchip headset and disc package. Another name was used. 'i' Telect. I understood it as an abbreviation for 'internet intellect.' A similar descriptive phrase was printed along side it. 'For mental improvement' was all it read. Simplified, it still bore the trademarks of the Occuchip brainwashing program. I must admit I felt a tad ill knowing it had gone into mass production and was most likely on a world wide market. God help us all.

Three-thirty came quick and I made my way through side streets and alleys until the thrift shop was in view. In the distance I could see Cloey talking to the preppy red head I'd the pleasure of meeting the night before. She was waiting for me. The smile I could not contain was quickly knocked out of me when out of the blue, I was hit from behind. Someone had smashed into me and sent me flying. I landed on the concrete and rolled with the kinetic energy. Swiftly I jumped to my feet to face my foe. My head spun but I forced myself to focus. One of the boys from last evening stood before me. "You shouldn't mess with our girls. It could be hazardous." He didn't grimace or raise his voice. The incandescence radiating from his stare told me why. He was infected. I had two choices. I could hang with Cloey and end up in a showdown with this guy or I could leave town. I wasn't about to back down even though it meant one of us would have to kill the other. How many more of his group had been struck with the illness? They could be planning attack and Cloey would be caught in the middle. I didn't wish to place her in an awkward position. It didn't matter what I wanted. The game was in motion and there'd be no winner. The kid made his move. Surprisingly he strolled away. When he vanished around the corner, I waited several minutes before heading to the safety of the thrift store. Cloey didn't see me approach and I took the opportunity to make sure I wasn't followed. "How was school?" I called when I was several feet away. She rushed over and hugged me. The red head looked on in disgust.

The familiar twinkle glistened in her eye. By now I was sure there were several bullets with my name on them. Perhaps it was jealousy that triggered the psychological change. An imbalance of electrolytes and cells brought on by emotional instability. I understood now a little of how the virus worked but was still perplexed as to why it was limited to certain individuals. "I have to go, Clove. See you at school tomorrow?" With one arm around my waist she replied, "Sure Cassy, first thing." She must've missed the narrowed glare as she turned her focus to me. Cassy stormed off, reminding me of Danny when he couldn't get his way. My stomach fluttered. I missed his company. I longed for the day I would see him again, whether in this realm or the next. "My friends aren't pleased with me hanging with you. They say you're a waste of my time." She pulled me close. "I don't think so." I was delighted by her candor even though the cold sensation of being observed hung stiffly in the air. "Nor I." I agreed. "Let's go inside."

We had spaghetti with home made monster balls for dinner. Monster balls meaning two inch thick meatballs with onion and spices. It's what Emma called them. She was a much better chef than mother. I wondered how they were getting along without me. Knowing mom she'd be convincing dad daily that I'd return any hour. As long as she was hopeful she'd be happy which would make his life much easier. Good enough reason for me to be glad for them and move on. I helped clear the dishes and Cloey washed and placed them in a drying rack. "How about we go for a stroll?" she asked when done. Of course I wanted to, but with the threat lurking about I chose against it. "I'm not sure that's such a good idea, you know, with your friends hating me and all." Her lip curled. "They don't hate you, silly. They just don't know you." "You mean they don't like me, don't you?" "That too." She concurred. "If we meet up with them you'll be safe. After all, you have me to protect you." "Don't take this the wrong way, but I don't believe you'd be much help. I believe they've been infected, at least one of the boys anyway. Cassy is too I suspect." Cloey leaned on the counter. "What makes you so sure?" I didn't wish to place my problems on her shoulder, but I thought it best to let her in on the day's events. "Glen wouldn't do that," was her first reaction when I told her of the threat I'd been handed. "I know he might not under normal circumstances, but who's to say he wouldn't if he was infected? I saw his expression. He's not who he was last night." "Well maybe we should go ask him," she snapped. I was losing the debate. She took my arm and dragged me toward the door. "Alright alright, let's forget about it. No need to stir up a hornets nest. If we meet up with him or any of them, you can decide then if I'm right." My nervousness ebbed and I took her in my arms. "In the meantime a romantic evening stroll couldn't hurt." So off we went. We held hands as we headed to a nearby park. The moon shone brightly beneath the cloudless sky, providing us plenty of light. Lamp posts lined the path, stealing any opportunity for an adversary to sneak up. A stagnant pond lay center of the gravel walkway. The occasional frog could be heard splashing off the shore, no doubt startled by our presence. I was glad to have dropped my defenses and even stopped listening for movement to the surrounding brush. We rested on a bench for nearly an hour, holding each other with the mutual admiration of long time lovers. Our one interruption came at seven o'clock when Cloey's cell phone rang. "That was Aunt Emma." She said as she closed it. "She wants us back so I can rest up for school. She worries too much." "Sounds as though she loves you." "Yeah," she agreed. "She does."

A short time later we were back at the thrift store. Cloey lay out our bed despite the cot and I took the opportunity to chat with Emma. "I don't feel safe with Clover out after dark, especially with the outbreak of recent murders. Just today I read of five more less than a hundred kilometers from here. The lower mainland has had almost fifty in the past few months. The virus is spreading fast." A shiver rippled through my spine. It was simply a matter of weeks or even days before the insurrection would flood this community. As it turned out it was much sooner. "I've bore witness to how the virus causes its victims to react. I'll keep a good watch over her for you. You've no need to worry. She'll be safe with me." Emma gave me an uncertain frown. Her concern was more than justified. "I'll take your word for it. Don't let me down." She ventured to the kitchen and I went over to check on Cloey. As the night before, sleeping bags were laid out with two pillows for our heads. She was nowhere in sight and I guessed she was in the washroom. I waited, looking over some jackets when I heard faint whispering coming from the next isle. I peered under the racks. Cloey was crouched with her back turned. Though I was nearly in reaching distance she hadn't heard me. Judging by the conversation she was having with her cell phone, one of her school pals was on the other line. Though she didn't name names, I figured it was Cassy. I picked up little of the subject they were on other than her whispers of "I can't" and "they can do it themselves, I want no part." My hunch was her group was planning something for me. What had I gotten her into? I snuck back to the dining room and waited for her. Emma arrived first with a plate of chocolate chip cookies.

I selected one and she sat across from me. I did my best to be of good cheer despite the circumstances. When I was down to the last bite, Cloey entered and sat beside me. She was obviously worried. "Is something wrong?" Emma asked. "Nothing I can't handle," she assured as she reached for a cookie. "Alright then, I'm going to bed. Clean up before you call it a night." When she was gone, Cloey began to cry. She dropped her cookie and lay her head on my shoulder. I didn't ask what was wrong, but wrapped my arms around her and lovingly stroked her hair. "You were right." She said after she calmed down. She lifted her head and stared intently into my soul. I caught the flash before the cascade of memories of past talks she had engaged in, including the last phone call. Pictures formed in my head and I understood her breakdown. They wanted me out of the way. Glen, Cassy, the whole lot wanted me away from her at all cost, even if it meant my death. It came as no surprise. "I see what you know Cloey. Don't be afraid. Read into me and know everything will be fine. I've overcome worse. We can overcome this." She stared a few seconds more than turned away. "You're right." She said without looking up. "We can handle this tomorrow. Better get some sleep." She pulled away and shuffled with her head down toward our bed. I stayed behind to clean up before joining her. Not once did she look into my face the rest of the night or the next morning.

# The Get—Away

When I raised my head the next day, I was unusually dizzy as though coming down with the flu. My stomach was queasy. My first instinct was to blame the amount of food I'd consumed from dinner on, though the pounding ache behind my eyes told me otherwise. My connection with Cloey, though spiritually enlightening had its own drawbacks and this was the beginning. Cloey was not beside me. I heard commotion in the dining area and assumed she and Emma were making breakfast. After a quick face wash and toilet break, I cleaned up the sleeping bags by folding and stacking them neatly with the other bedding. "Sure slept late, didn't you?" Emma chimed as I entered the kitchen. There was no disappointment in her tone. "I suppose." I answered while glancing around for Cloey. She wasn't there. "What time is it?" "Almost one. You slept over twelve hours. Cover left for school around seven. She told me not to wake you." Almost one? The connection had deeper impact than imagined. "What about the store?" I asked. "You may have lost customers because of me." She set a bowl and box of bran flakes on the counter and took a spoon from the cutlery drawer. "Don't worry. I'm closed for the day. Got paperwork to do. I know you'll want to pick up Clover after school, but in the meantime, if you want to clean up around here, you can earn some cash. Sweep and mop the shop, kitchen and dining room and I'll give you fifty bucks. You can take Clover somewhere special for dinner." Wow, I thought. The job shouldn't take more than an hour and a half. I could meet Cloey at three if I hurried. "Deal!" I blurted out in excitement. "Okay then. Eat up, do your dishes and get started. When you're done come to my office. It's right over there." She pointed to an unmarked door across the four-tabled dining hall and strolled to it. When she reached it she turned and said, "You'll find the mop, soap and bucket in the woman's washroom. Bathroom floors are included." She smiled and in that moment I caught not only a compassion rarely seen, but an abnormal sadness deep in her heartfelt gaze. I thought of what it must be like for a long lost loved one to return home. I figured she felt that way of me due to my bond with her niece, though it didn't explain the sorrow. That, I would discover later.

In an hour and fifteen minutes the floors were done. The mop and bucket were washed and returned and I headed for the office. Emma didn't hear me advance. She was shoving cash into a white envelope. When she was done I waited for her to seal it. She wrote something on the backside and slid it under a tray marked 'outgoing mail'. I stepped back several paces so she wouldn't know I'd seen her and called, "All done." She met me at the door, and handed me two twenties and a ten. "I'll check your work out later, but from where I'm standing, you've done a good job." She pointed to the chairs I'd set inverted on the table edges. "Those you can leave as is. Most people who clean for me slide them aside. You're the first in a while to use common sense. You'll need that skill in the future, now go. Clover's waiting. Scoot." She ushered me to the rear door. "Have fun." She said as she closed and locked it. I couldn't help but sense a nervous urgency in her mannerisms, but dismissed them at the time. Cloey was expecting me at her school.

I hadn't yet laid a foot on the school grounds when I spotted them. They walked side by side in military fashion directly toward me. Cloey led the group of five, a step ahead of the other four. When they were about four paces away they stopped. Cassy spoke first. Not to me, but Cloey. "Go ahead," she nudged Cloey and crossed her arms like the others. Cloey held her hands on her hips. Her chin was up and a distasteful pout marked her intention. "What's going on?" I asked with iron sullenness. I knew the answer but needed to hear it from her. "Tell him." Cassy pressured. "Yeah," Glen but in. "Tell him what's on your mind." I wanted to smash that self righteous smirk off his face permanently. I knew whatever Cloey had to say, they had put her up to it. I searched her face for some truth to my belief and came up empty. She was either hiding it well or no longer cared for me. I questioned myself if she ever had or had Occuchip cleverly planned for me this grief. "I don't want to see you anymore." She spat. "You don't belong here." She turned to the group then again to me. "These are my friends," she continued. "And this is where I belong. Do yourself a favor and leave town." Justin stepped up and wrapped his arm around her waist. "Yeah, leave tonight." The lightning flashed over his pupils. His expression remained neutral. "Before something bad happens." He leaned in and kissed her lips . . . Until that moment I didn't know what blind rage was or felt like. Until it swept through me I didn't believe it actually existed, but at that moment I was consumed. It happened so fast I had no idea I'd even moved. One second, I was standing, staring dumbfounded and the next I had Justin by the throat. I was pounding his face, swinging my fist back and forth like a pendulum across his cheeks, eyes and nose. Glen and the other boy grabbed me and hauled me off before throwing me down and kicking my arms and ribs. Cassy had let out a blood chilling shriek which drew the attention of every student and teacher within ear shot. I heard someone yell 'fight' which took attention off me. I took the opportunity to scramble to my feet. Justin stayed on the ground holding his nose with one hand, while propping himself with the other. Blood leaked through his fingers. His friends helped him up. Students came jogging over. Most turned to leave when they saw the fight had ended. I turned to leave too, but Cloey blocked my path. "Good girl." Justin called. "You're not going anywhere." To my shock, Cassy intervened. "Let it go Justin, it's over." He stepped toward me. She shoved him back. "I said it's over. You got what you want, now let it go." I faced Cloey. Never had I felt more betrayed. She still wore the bitch pout. "Well?" She looked away and stepped aside. There was no need to look over my shoulder. I had made up my mind I was leaving town that night. I would ask Emma to pack me a lunch before I gathered my belongings and headed on my way.

The rear door to the thrift store stood ajar. The place was deathly quiet. I crept inside and called Emma's name. There was no response other than the steady hum of the refrigerator. I crossed from the kitchen into the dining area. Chairs from two of the tables lay strewn about the floor and scuff marks announced there'd been a struggle. Drag patterns from rubber shoe soles led to the office. I pictured the concerned expression on Emma and the haste in which she shuffled me to the exit as I inched forth. As I reached the door, I noticed Emma's foot sticking out as though she were reclining. When I popped my head in there she was, propped in the chair. Bruises on her neck pointed to strangulation, but her stomach area was drenched in blood. There was no object protruding from the puncture so I assumed the killer or killers had taken it. "She's dead isn't she?" I whirled around to see who'd snuck up on me, but even before I saw her face, her voice had given her away. The sarcastic, snotty snarl had changed to a sympathetic frown. "I thought you'd be with your friends where you belong. Are they waiting outside? I guess my turn's coming isn't it?" "It's not like that." She said in defense. "You have no idea what I've done for you." "Done for me?" I snapped. "You referring to my betrayal or the moment you broke my heart? Yeah, you've done plenty alright." "I had no choice. They would've killed us both. You were right, they're all infected and they're not the only ones. Half the school's been brainwashed. If I hadn't made it look real they wouldn't have let me go and I'd never have seen you again." I turned to face the corpse who used to be a caring woman. Someone uncorrupted by this decaying world, killed for her inability to conform to evil and wise enough to sacrifice herself for us. I knew I was next and wished enough wisdom had been passed on so I would stand up when the time came. I wondered how well she knew her attackers and if she trusted them as I had Cloey. Who would wield the blade intent on taking **me** down? Cloey grabbed my arm and I whirled around. I had startled her enough she let go and stepped away. "I sacrificed for you just as she did for us." She knew what I was thinking. Was it possible or a lucky guess? "I won't let them kill you. They won't take another person I love." Humbly she lowered her eyes to the floor. She knew I had a tough time believing her. I had to know for sure. "Look at me." I pushed her chin up. "Let me see for myself." It took an instant before she gazed back, and in that second the twinkle appeared along with her intimate thoughts. She truly had stuck her neck out for me though it went against every fiber of her being. Still, one thing puzzled me. If I could see she was faking, why couldn't they? "They didn't look directly at me. I wouldn't let them. Please forgive me." The way she read my thoughts was unnerving. Whereas I could see in part what she allowed, she could read me like a book. I was about to ask how, but I had no need. She answered before I could speak. "Remember you were rejected. You received only part of the program, but that's not all. I seem to be the only one I know who can read minds, but only yours. I had no idea if the others knew I was faking or not and was puzzled when you couldn't tell otherwise. We were meant to find each other. We are meant to be together. How could you not see the incredible bond we share?" I could see it. Sure I could. My problem was believing her. My perception of truth had become cloudy by the lies I was sure were fact. I couldn't allow myself to fall into a similar trap, though I knew if I didn't let my guard down soon, I might end up tossing away the most important opportunity I'd been given. She did a great job deceiving me for our benefit. The least I could do was allow her to continue to prove herself. Time would decide whose side she played for. "You really hurt me." I began. I would not make eye contact for obvious reasons. I couldn't give her ammunition in case I was wrong. "That's not easy to let go, but you came to me and didn't have to. So either you're a great actress or in love with me. Seeing that your classmates haven't shown up, I'll take your word. Of course you know they'll hunt you down too." "I'm not afraid." She wrapped me in her embrace and I accepted. It felt good to have her warm body close to mine. Again I was no longer alone. "We'll have to leave tonight." I told her. "Your aunt paid me fifty bucks to clean up. We can use it to get by for a few days." She pushed away and held me at arms length. "Alright, but fifty dollars won't go far. Auntie Emma said she had emergency money put away for me. She said if anything happened to her it would be easy to find. All I had to do was be outgoing enough to search for it." My mind raced back to the last time I saw Emma alive and to the envelope she hid. "Outgoing as in outgoing mail. I saw her stuff an envelope under the mail tray." Cloey pushed by me and entered the office. A soft whimper escaped her upon sight of her aunt. I followed to give comfort. "My friends didn't do this." She exclaimed. "It was someone else. Someone who knows you're here." I had no idea who it could've been and frankly I didn't want to know. I'd be happy just to be away from here. "The money, Cloey. Hurry. I have a bad feeling." It wasn't so much a negative emotion that prompted my fight or flight response, but the claustrophobia setting in. There weren't too many exits in this building and my enemies could arrive any moment. Cloey lifted the mail tray and took the envelope. "This is it. It has my name on it." She was about to open it but I stopped her. "No, not yet. Gather some clothes, bathroom supplies . . . anything you need that's light enough to carry long distance. Feminine products as well if you have them. The less we need to shop for, the better. I'll gather some food. There's enough room in my pack for a few meals." I headed for the kitchen. "Wait." "Yes Cloey?" I was in such a frenzy to get out of there I had to bite my tongue to refrain from snapping. I'm glad now I did. "Thank you.

You know, for believing me." She had the same sheepish grin as when I complimented her beautiful name. It was as though we had started over. "Hurry," I said. "We'll talk more later."

In less than twenty minutes we were on our way. Cloey had found a camouflage camping pack that included a rack that a sleeping bag could be tied to. I had no idea how skilled she was at packing the essentials. It was apparent she'd gone camping several times. Being a gentleman I traded with her as my pack was considerably lighter. Cautiously we made our way through town being as inconspicuous as possible. Unfortunately the route she'd planned led us to wooded trails behind the high school. Call me crazy but I followed her lead. She did know the town better than I which gave us an advantage. Around the school we headed, aiming for the cluster of fir trees or pines, whichever they were. When we reached the trail she stopped and held her hand up. "You notice something?" she whispered as she peered over her shoulder toward the school. I hadn't spotted anything out of the ordinary. "Yeah," I mumbled in response. "We're safe. There's no one around here." Maintaining her low tone she asked, "Exactly. Don't you think it strange we haven't seen at least one student hanging around?" I saw her point. School day or no, someone would be either using the field or otherwise hanging about. It was only four-thirty and the sun was high in the sky. "Where could they be?" I asked out loud. We began our march through the woods. "Who knows." She spoke with less hesitation as though satisfied we were safe. "How about right here?" The voice came from behind. We whirled around in time to spot Justin stepping from behind a tree. His face was badly bruised and his nose was crooked. I must've broken it. He behaved as though he was in no pain regardless. He held his hands out of sight behind him and I told myself he was holding his hand gun. "We're **all** here." He exclaimed. His pupils lit up but the spark didn't fade. "Stay close." I grabbed Cloey's arm and pulled her to my side. There was an ominous shuffling that came from all directions and the next thing I knew, we were surrounded by at least twelve students. Some I recognized from the computer lab. All their eyes held the same fluorescent white glow. "I was going to ask you to be part of our group again, Cloey, but I see you've made you choice." Cassy joined him and kissed his cheek. "I've made mine." He whispered in her ear. I'm no lip reader by any standard but it was obvious what two words he said, 'kill her.' Cassy began to walk toward us. The other teens stood as sentinels, determined not to let us leave. I felt a nudge to my ribs and Cloey told me to stand aside. To honor her wish I did but I stayed poised to defend if needed. "Too bad you chose him over us." Her eyes narrowed slightly, but other than that her blank, dead guise remained the same. Cloey hid her hand beneath her sweater. "We could have ruled this town together." She pulled something from her waist band. Cassy was three steps away when the gun came up with the barrel to her face. She stopped dead. "I suggest you go home, all of you." Cloey was returning the evil eye she'd given me to her previous best friends. Justin moved closer with deliberately slow steps. His hands came up in surrender. My intuition was correct. The pistol he'd drawn on me at our first encounter was in his right hand. He kept the barrel up. "You gonna shoot your friend, Cloey? You really wanna do that?" He took another step. She swung the gun his way and grasped the grip with both hands. "If I have to." She said. "You'll have to." Cassy snarled. She lunged for Cloey's weapon. Instinctively Cloey turned to her and fired. As instantly as the shot rang out, Cassy's eyes returned to normal. Her hands clutched her chest below her right breast as a look of disbelief transformed her dead features. She dropped to her knees. Justin brought the gun to head level. He was aiming for me. I jumped aside as the shot echoed through the trees, followed by another. I glanced up in time to watch him collapse face first. Arms sprawled, he didn't move. Cloey swung the gun around to let the others know whoever moved first was next. "Get outta here!" she screamed. "All of you." The students were dumbfounded and began backing away. They all were somewhat normal again. Soon they were gone and we were left with Justin and Cassy. Cloey rushed over to Justin to retrieve his revolver while I hurried to Cassy's side. She was on her back, choking and spitting blood. "Where's Cloey?" She stammered. "I have to . . ." She rolled over and coughed up more blood. I have to say I felt pity for her. Cloey checked Justin's vitals before joining us. "He's dead. Here, take his gun." I grabbed it and flipped the drum open. There were two other bullets other than the spent shell. I popped one out. The slug end was crimped. They were blanks. "This won't do us any good." I said as I tossed it into the trees. Cloey trained her gun on Cassy. "Don't let it change you." Cassy choked. Don't let it win. You're on its list, both of you. It wants you dead." She lay on her side and closed her eyes. Tears welled in ours as we observed her life slip away. "I never wanted this." Cloey mumbled through heavy sobs. "Neither of us did. We have to go." She nodded and wiped her tears with her sleeve. I helped her to her feet.

"Where did you find this?" I asked in reference to the 22 caliber pistol. According to Cloey's instinct, we were an hour northwest of her town. She hadn't said much from the time we left Cassy's side until now. Like me she likely wondered what brought us from our secluded and protected lives to the point of abandoning two murdered school chums on a wooded hillside. She may have been dwelling on the fact she was now a wanted fugitive with two deaths on her conscience. How could one computer program change so many lives so negatively? It was as though the heavens had opened and dumped the biblical revelation on us. This was the end times. The antichrist, nothing more than a simple electronic virus and we were man's last hope. Some hope. We were as lost as confused. Even violence was thrust upon us despite all effort to avoid it. "Auntie Emm kept it in the store behind the counter. She hated guns. Uncle Vic gave it to her. I don't know why she kept it. I guess it was a reminder of him." "Where is he now?" She held her hand out and I gave the weapon back. "Dead. He was killed in a car accident two years ago. A drunk driver crossed the center line. He didn't stand a chance. Can we talk about something else?" She shoved the cold steel into her waist band. Why she chose to carry it so close was beyond me. She had to have been spooked more than I imagined. "Why did you toss the revolver?" She inquired. How could I tell her it was loaded with blanks? Knowing she was in no real danger of being shot could push her over the edge, so I lied. "The cartridges were spent. He must've fired the last one. Lucky for us." "Yeah," she sighed. "Lucky." We continued through the wilderness on service roads and trails until twilight. The clear sky gave indication it would be a dry night and we searched for a suitable place to set up camp. As it was, we happened upon a hunter's cabin. Inside was a wood stove and cot. Though the floor was filthy we chose it as a bed. The cot was too small for us both, so we used it to spread out our gear. "What do we do for a bathroom?" Cloey finally broke the silence. I saw what could have been an outhouse around back and I told her I'd clear it of cob webs if she set up our dinner. She agreed. While I dusted the webs from the entrance, I realized we had little water. Two half liter bottles to be exact. It would do until morning. There was no toilet seat, only a hole roughly cut by a jigsaw. No toilet paper either. Cloey should've packed it. I cleared the hole of web strands and when I was satisfied she'd be pleased, I went back to the cabin. Cloey had the camouflage bag dumped out and was rummaging through its contents. "I brought us each a toothbrush in case you didn't bring one." She held up a pack of matches. "Fire?" She asked. I told her no. Our food didn't need warming. Left over sandwiches and fruit is all I packed and we would be warm enough not to require extra heat. I also didn't want to risk attracting unwanted attention. She shrugged, replaced them and scooped up a box of 22 shells. "Might as well reload, we may need it again." After exchanging two cartridges, she installed the clip and put the rest away.

Egg sandwiches an apple and water was our dinner. Afterward, Cloey grabbed a roll of toilet paper off the cot and headed outside. I knew she'd remember to bring it. It was a woman thing. A handful of tissue paper or paper towel could last me days, unlike mom who could run through a roll in one. I jokingly pondered on how long that one roll would last and if it would be noticeably smaller when she came back. I wish I'd brought a book along to fill in the drawn out minutes. It had to have been more than a half an hour when my patience finally wore thin. I was worried something might have happened to my girl, so I went out to find her. I first checked the obvious place, the outhouse. She wasn't there but the toilet paper was. I couldn't see a difference in the size of the roll which showed me she wasn't wasteful like mom. I loved that about her. I decided to wander the tree line. She could be clearing her head by taking a break from me. "Cloey." I called. She didn't answer right away which really put my nerves on edge. For all I knew we could've been followed and she could be resting in a shallow grave. I called again and perked my ears in anticipation. I heard nothing at first other than the soft wind rustling the branches and the chipper trill of songbirds. Then there it was, the soft whimper emanating from behind a tree. I circled around and found Cloey with her head down. She had propped her back against the trunk and was staring into the gun barrel. "Cloey, what are you doing?" Her reply sent chills through me. "Deciding when to end your burden." "What do you mean?" I quietly asked. I was really worried at this point.

"You know what I mean. You said it yourself. You can't trust me. I've lied to you and even though my intentions were well meaning, we'll never be close like before. I hoped I could prove myself to you by leaving together, but it didn't work. I made things worse. Now I'm a killer too." She took a deep breath and continued. As she spoke my heart went out to her and I understood her anguish. "They didn't have to die. Cassy was unarmed and Justin's gun held blanks." So she knew all along. Perhaps she tested me to see how far I'd go to protect her. She lifted her head. "I shot him anyway. So you should understand why I have to do this . . ." She placed the barrel under her chin. My heart skipped a beat and I froze. "You see, I must be infected. No rational person would do what I did. I have to make things right." "Please." I begged as I dropped to my knees. "Don't blame yourself. I know you're not infected. You've been given some difficult choices and handled them as best you could." "No!" she insisted. "You don't understand. I broke your heart for no reason. I didn't have to listen to them. We could've run away. I knew Justin never put real bullets in his gun. I shot him anyway. Even Cassy said I was infected. Why do you think she told us not to let it win? It can only kill us if we let it because it isn't out there, it's in us and I gave into it." She lay her head against the tree. I reached over to wipe a tear off her cheek but she pushed my arm away. "Don't touch me, I'm toxic." I know I should've kept my cool and remained low key, but something about her stubbornness told me it would be futile. I was angry, not at her but with the hell this virus inflicted. It was the master mind game. If it couldn't infect us, it would lie and make us question ourselves. It could destroy us without even trying. It was making sense that it was more than a mere infection, it was an unholy conscience. An enemy without its own body. The devil going under the assumed name of Occuchip. "Don't you see what's happening here?" I barked. "You're letting it win by giving up. Whatever you did is done. You had decisions to make and you made them, right or wrong. No one in your position would do much else. It's called survival and you did what you had to. With all my heart I forgive you. I know the struggle you're facing. Stop blaming yourself. I love you . . ." Slowly she twisted her head to face me. She seemed stunned as if I'd slapped her. "What?" She asked as she leaned closer. She laid the gun on the soft dirt and blinked. "You mean that? You don't hate me?" "Of course not." I took her hands in mine. They were cold like the dull black steel of the 22. "Can't you see it? Doesn't it reflect in the windows of my soul? Without you I'd be hollow and aimless. Since meeting you, it's like my life has found purpose. If you knew how lost I'd be without you, you wouldn't feel so alone. Don't give up. I'd lose everything I have to live for." Tears stopped flowing at that point. We held each other until the shadows of night fell upon us. During that hour she confessed a secret shared not only by her school, but the whole town. After the first few displays of violence, the Occuchip program had been banned. Everyone knew it after several announcements from the mayor. For a week it was stressed through television, radio and newspaper how dangerous it could be and that every headset and disc should be destroyed. The principal in his infinite wisdom chose to keep one in the lab as his own experiment. When the results of the first month showed no adverse effects, the mayor allowed the study to continue. Students were closely monitored and required weekly physicals by their assigned physicians. Any students who dropped out of the class were exempt and free to carry on with no supervision. When the first student showed signs of mental illness he was taken away and treated at an institution. Word was he never left, nor the few who followed after. Because of the high success rate, the project was allowed to advance. "I quit computer lab when we met." Cloey told me. "I guess it was because I saw how mistreated you were. I didn't want to take a chance at becoming conformed to a specific way of thinking. I valued the individuality I saw in you. Now that I see how far I could have gone, I'm glad I did." "I'm shocked they would ever consider putting so many youth at risk. After all the murders you'd think they would've shut it all down." "They didn't care. Parents were proud to have intellectual children, even if it meant facing the direst of consequences. Our town is so snobbish." I had to agree.

# Forget Me Not

I woke before Cloey and quickly dressed for my trip to the outhouse. The sun was fairly low in the east. I guessed it to be around seven-thirty or eight. The minimal sunlight which permeated the trees dissolved the cold air as well as my concerns for the future. I took the solace as a time to be thankful. Despite the insanity all over this province I knew as B.C., I was one of the few to avoid it, if only for a short while. I thanked whatever holy presence guided me, for my companion and a wonderful sunny day. On my way from the latrine I heard a commotion coming from the cabin. I hoped Cloey would have a sandwich and kiss ready. I couldn't have been more wrong. I opened the door and showed my appreciation of her with a gentle smile. She greeted me back with the business end of the 22. "Who . . . who are you?" She stammered as she backed against the far wall by the foot of the cot. "What am I doing here?" I would've thought she was putting me on had she grinned or put the gun down. She did neither, which threw me on the defensive. She flicked off the safety which proved she meant business. "Come on Cloey, you know me. Ben, remember?" She shot me a perplexed frown. I lowered to my knees. "We left town last night." I was about to remind her of her dead friends but thought it may do more damage than good. Whatever programming she ingested was toying with her memory. I hoped the damage wouldn't be permanent or irreversible. "A computer program has gotten into our heads. Not just ours, but much of your town. Remember telling me of it last night? Your school held a class which used headsets to directly link the students' minds to the software." I was getting nowhere. How much more could I explain? I wasn't sure if I should try later or continue. I took a deep breath and thought of key words that may jog a recent memory. Headset, computer, programming . . . Then the sun came through the small pane-less window and shone in my eyes. I had to blink and turn away. Of course! How could I have been so stupid? I forgot about our deepest connection. Now if only I could make long enough eye contact for it to work. I said a silent prayer in hopes she'd remember and I wouldn't forget as she. "Look at me." She was staring my way but not at my face. "Come on." I said. "If you're gonna shoot me you may as well look me in the eye." The ploy worked. "Now Cloey, try to understand I don't wish you harm. We are good friends. We're traveling as a pair." Something spooked her and she hid her face. The virus wouldn't let me in. I had no choices left and I took the biggest gamble of my life. I rushed at her. Catching my movement she swung around. I reached for the pistol and grabbed her wrist instead. A shot rang out and I landed on top of her, pinning her down. My heart was pumping, pounding against my ribcage. I felt the heat of the burning gun powder and the sting of the bullet as it brushed by my cheek. "Get off of me!" She screamed while violently thrashing to escape. I slammed her wrist to the floor while reaching for the other. The gun fell free and I wiggled my way up her torso. I was able to pin one arm under my knee which left me with a free hand. Being careful not to squeeze her throat, I clamped on her jaw and forced her head straight. "Look at me." I demanded. As futile as it was she continued to struggle under my weight. "I said get OFF!" Her scream was shrill enough to shatter glass and my ear drums paid the price. "Stop it." I yelled back. "Quit being so damned stubborn. Look at me or so help you, I'll peel your eyelids back. Do it!" I don't fully comprehend what happened right then as she relented her fight. Her body went limp beneath me with far less effort than anticipated. As I mulled over her bizarre behavior, I began to see more of Cloey's true personality. Her eyes popped open and a calming wave seemed to sweep over her. The virus had lost the battle. Somewhere deep within she was able to muster up enough will power to restrain it. Perhaps it knew how vain its effort was. Either way she was co-operating. "Much better." I cooed. An electrical impulse filled my head as transfer began. As though rebooting a hard drive my memories poured into her glowing retinas. Her body twitched from what I understood to be stimulation of the cerebrum and cerebellum. Yes, I too took biology. When her pupils ceased shining my job was done. Cloey still lay motionless other than the odd twitch in her fingers and neck. "How do you feel?" I asked as she attempted to elevate herself. The gun was still at her side and she caught me glancing toward it. "How did I get over here, Ben? Why do my wrists hurt?" Good, she remembered who I was. She lay against the log wall. "I'm so tired. Where are we?" Okay, so not all of her memories were intact, but hey, she knew who I was. That meant more to me. The rest we could work on. "What's the last thing you remember?" I moved in and she reached for the 22. I held still while she took it by both hands and examined it. "This. I was gonna shoot myself, but then you came. You talked me down. Why can't I remember anything else? Tell me, how did we get here? Where **is** here?" I took a better part of half an hour to explain. Like me she couldn't recall where home was or how to return. Unfortunately the deaths of her school buddies lingered and the guilt flooded in. Once the circumstances were re-explained, she settled into the girl she was the night before. "Come on, we have to pack up. We'll have breakfast before we leave. The next community shouldn't be too far away. Could you count how much your aunt gave you?" "My aunt?" Her confusion got me to thinking 'here we go again', but thankfully I didn't have to. "Oh yeah, I almost forgot." She dug through her clothes bag and pulled out the envelope. She tore the end open and dumped the bills into her palm. "Wow" I exclaimed. "That's a lot of cash." No bill was less then a twenty. The wad consisted of mostly hundreds and fifties. The sum total came to three thousand, six hundred dollars. A sizeable gift and one heck of a good start. She fanned out the money and waved it over her face. "You're not gonna faint are you?" "Of course not." She giggled. It was good to see her care free again.

# Hell Town

Despite our exhaustion after a four hour hike and the hunger and thirst that constantly gnawed at us, we were in relatively high spirits. We were fortunate enough to catch a glimpse of many a forest animal, including deer, chipmunks, a cougar and a mother bear with two cubs. The cougar was in a tree across from a grassy field we had entered. Cloey spotted it first and latched on to my arm. Her concern was ending up on its menu, which I could understand. I told her if we kept walking and acknowledged its presence by talking to it, we would be safe. It was humorous to listen to her babble on about love and respect for nature and how poorly we'd taste if it desired a snack. When we met up with the bears on the far side of the same plateau, she really freaked and hid behind me with arms around my waist. I told her to use the same technique, only this time she resorted to begging for them to ignore us. The mother stood on its haunches and sniffed the air but was relatively unconcerned by our presence. That came as little relief and I'm sure I ended up with bruised ribs. From the grassland we came upon a jagged slope which overlooked a valley. From there we could see roads and farm houses. A bustling highway lay just beyond so we headed for it. "East or west Cloe, your choice." She pointed west and exclaimed, "First thing we do is rent a hotel. I need a shower bad." I'm glad she chose west. East would've taken us close to her old town. "Yeah, me too." We continued on to the overpass less than three city blocks from where we met the highway. We chose to hitchhike and in no time a middle aged man picked us up. "Nice car." Cloey commented as she climbed onto the leather front seat of the Mercedes. "Yeah," I agreed "nice". I rode in the back. "I can take you as far as the next city." He sized up Cloey. "That's where we're going." I said to divert his attention. Cloey nervously shifted in her seat. Something about the guy wasn't right. "Don't I know you two from somewhere?" he asked. "I don't know." Cloey stared at her lap. "Sure I do." The stranger lowered his voice to a menacing tone. "You're Clover Riley. I've been looking for you." She swallowed hard and her breathing came shallow and quick. "I'm a friend of your aunt Emma." His cold stare penetrated my defenses as he glared through the rear view. I kicked myself for convincing Cloey to keep the gun in the pack when we neared civilization. It was doubtful I'd be able to reach it if this guy made a false move. I couldn't stand the tension any longer and blurted. "Then you must know Uncle Vic." "Sure do." He said through a phony smile. "Why just last week we were discussing how mature you've been getting, Clover." He wouldn't keep me in the discussion which gave me the creepy idea I wouldn't be ending the ride with them. How he knew Emma was beyond me, for if he did, he'd know Uncle Vic was dead. I played along if for nothing more than to distract him from Cloey. "Fishing trip, right? Vic loves to fish." Whether he did or not I had no clue. I just wanted to see how far this guy would go. "That's right, me, my dad and Vic. Dad knew your uncle when you were just a small fry." We were nearing the exit to the next town. "Then you must have a few good stories to tell." He didn't seem to notice or care as I dug through Cloey's belongings. I was feeling mighty grateful she'd handed me her bag before climbing in. "Well I'm sure I got a few." He signaled and pulled to the side of the road several hundred yards before the exit. As he braked my hand fell on the barrel and I carefully slid it out and kept it low. "I'm more interested in yours." The car jerked to a stop and he turned to me. I heard something click and Cloey gasped. "He . . . he's got a gun, Ben." "Shut up." The man snapped. She cowered by the door. Her petrified whimpering gave the impression she knew who this character was. I was busy putting two and two together and came up with the simplest solution. This guy knew Cloey's aunt but not the uncle. That was obvious, but what infuriated me was **how** he knew her. He had killed Emma and now it was our turn. "Get out. Clover's coming with me. Be thankful I'm letting you live." "You bastard." I huffed and pressed the 22 into the soft leather of his seat. "You'll kill her like her aunt." He chuckled. "Not until we download what she knows. You see a group of us want to put an end to these irritating glitches in certain people's programming. People like her have the answer. We're gonna find it." "What about me?" I asked. My finger rested on the trigger. "I'm no different. You don't see me acting crazy, do you?" He threw his head back as he laughed. "You just don't get it, do you? What grade level are you at, seven, eight? See where I'm going with this? Your program didn't take. If anything, you're more stupid than before, now get out." Stupid huh? I was so angry I had no retort but one. "Screw you." And those were his trigger words. He brought the gun up and over the seat and I snapped off two rounds before he could train it on me. He dropped the larger handgun and turned back to the road. Cloey was fighting with the door handle. "It's locked!" She cried. I reached over the seat and hit the lock release on the driver door handle. "Try it now." The door swung open. I pushed her seat forward when she climbed out and handed her our supplies. I crawled out after and then pushed the seat to its upright position. The stranger's breathing was shallow. "Son of a bitch", he spat as I reached for his gun. "I think I'm paralyzed." If he wasn't, he'd be dead soon enough. I don't know where the projectile struck, but the back of his white tee shirt was saturated a deep crimson. "Not bad for grade seven-eight education." I sneered. He tilted his head my way. "It's not over." He choked. "Not by a long shot." The haunting sparkle leaped at me through his death stare and faded. Briefly I caught a glimpse of what he meant. As his vitals faded I realized as bad as things were they could get much worse.

Midway into the foreign city we found a decrepit dive bearing a hotel sign. Before checking in Cloey asked how long we would stay. I recommended two nights to give us time to plan our next move. She paid the clerk and we headed to the second floor. The room was small as expected with a double bed and bureau using most of the living space. A hanging picture of a vase of roses hung over the bed. Because it was crooked the white paint beneath was exposed, showing the years of nicotine build-up. It dulled the rest of the room a yellow brown. The bed was made but had a musty smell. Either the room hadn't been used for a while or the bedding hadn't been washed. I suggested we lay our sleeping bag over the comforter. Cloey toured the bathroom while I picked out some clean clothes. "No soap or shampoo." She didn't sound too surprised and neither was I. "Good thing I packed some." She joined me in the next room and took a quick look around. "Wow, a hot plate. How fitting. Do you suppose the butter knives have scorched ends?" "Not if they're plastic." I jested. "No fridge and the T.V. must be ancient. Doesn't matter, I didn't order it hooked up. Can you believe they want fifty a night **and** extra for cable? It's outrageous." I stopped what I was doing and embraced her. "That's okay hon. There's probably nothing good on anyhow." I rubbed my hands up and down her back. She smiled and kissed me. "So I suppose we're showering separately?" I had to ask. "Not if I can help it." She replied with a wink.

Before our shower, we made love. I expected to be awkward, seeing as I was a virgin. She had some experience which I expected and our movements were fluid and natural. After we lay for a while, holding each other until hunger prompted us to get up. "You think they have room service?" I sarcastically asked. "They don't even have a phone to order pizza." I got dressed and dug the fifty from my pocket. "Dinner is on me. It was your aunt's wish. I'd like to honor it." The mention of Emma brought reality flooding in. I was on edge again, wondering if the police or another infected individual would track us down. Cloey too was feeling the pinch and automatically went somber. Lost in her own hell, she reached for her gun. She took the silver nine millimeter I'd taken from the stranger and handed it to me. "We're fugitives," she said. "We might as well get used to it. Check the clip." She had to show me the release. She too checked hers. "There are two shots missing." She lowered her brow. "There should be only one. What happened to the other?" She'd forgotten about the struggle in the cabin. My hand went to my cheek where the bullet grazed it, leaving a shallow scratch. "It discharged by mistake sometime during your black-out at the cabin. No harm done." "Well, okay," she mumbled. "How many rounds do you have?" I flicked the shells from the clip and counted. "I have eight." "Good," she replaced the two and slapped the clip into the handle. "Nearly full, hurry and reload, dear. I'm starving."

We left everything we owned other than the guns and money in the hotel and walked to the nearest café. We each order a burger, fries and a soft drink. After, we toured a second hand store for a purse for Cloey. She said it would be easier on us to carry a small amount of supplies including the weapons, in case of an emergency. I agreed, being as I was done with carrying the damn thing in my waistband. I was tired of it digging into me when I moved certain ways and she made it clear she felt the same. We, or rather she, found a suitable handbag for eight bucks. Outside in the nearest alley, we off loaded and she put the bag on her shoulder. "How's it look?" "Great." I told her. "Handy too." We toured the area the rest of the day, taking advantage of our time. We explored a few trailed areas and ate granola bars on a park bench. We drank bottled water and chased ducks and geese which chose to rest along the edge of a stagnant pond. We were free to feel alive and shake off stress. We walked for the better part of the day and planned on finding a rental suite to settle down in. Sure we'd have to be diligent in our dealings with the public and keep up on local news. Any hint the heat was on us and we'd disappear. That was our plan. Back in the hotel we sat on the bed and read the newspaper. There was no report of the stranger or any recent murders. Our guards began to drop. We settled in for the night, grateful to be safe.

Sometime in the middle of the night, I awoke to a thump. It came from down the hall. Voices followed and I heard someone say 'B6', our room number. Instantly I was wide awake and shaking Cloey. "Get up," I told her. "Someone's coming, we've gotta move fast." We barely finished putting on our clothes when the lock clicked and the door flew open. Cloey grabbed her purse and dove beside the bed. Before I could react, three men in dark clothes burst in. They brandished automatic weapons and wore ski masks. "Where's your money?" The first one in said as he shoved the rifle in my face. The other two searched the bathroom and bureau. None of them noticed Cloey. She'd crawled under the bed. "It's not here." Somehow they must've found out about Emma's gift. "I've got nearly thirty dollars." I reached for my pockets and was struck across the face with the barrel of my intimidators cannon. I fell to the foot of the bed. Blood dripped from my nose. Glen would have laughed at the irony had he known. "Get up, you piece of crap." The gunman tugged my shirt and hauled me to my feet. "Check under the bed," he commanded the partner closest to him. The other stood guard at the door. My assailant wouldn't take his eyes off mine. I know he hadn't used the poisoned program, for his eyes revealed nothing of its affect. He was normal despite his obvious stupidity. These guys were no pros. Crack heads with guns is all they were, sent out by their source to rob us of a measly three grand. Cloey had more sense than they and she proved it right then. The thief crouched beside the bed. He reached his hand under first and felt for the envelope. I could imagine how close he came to brushing by Cloey. "I don't feel it." He said. He was about to stand when the leader barked. "Put your head to the floor, idiot. If you don't see it, check beneath the mattress." He did as he was told much to his regret. A sharp pop like a muffled fire cracker broke the silence. As 'idiot' crumpled another resounded and the guy by the door let out a shriek. He too fell over, grabbing at his ankle. It was all the distraction I needed. Their leader turned away.

'Good aim, girl.' I thought as I grabbed the gun and yanked it from his weakened grip. He turned to me in time for the butt to smash his upper teeth. It was enough to knock him out. I held the rifle on the thug by the door. He was the only one moving. The guy with his face under the bed was obviously dead. Cloey confirmed when she crawled out the other side. "You never cease to amaze me." I told her. She grinned, stepped over the one I knocked out and glared at the one she shot in the foot. "Who sent you?" she pried. "Screw you." He whimpered. "Fine, don't answer. Ben, fill my shoulder bag with what we need." She kicked her victim in the head. It snapped back hard and he collapsed. "We're leaving here now." I was impressed by her protective instinct. I didn't know she could be so brutal. Having nothing to lose could do that to a person. "Remind me never to piss you off." She simply said, "I just did. How's the nose?" It no longer bled. "I'll be okay, how bad does it look?" She grimaced and replied, "I'm sure it'll be fine once you wash the blood off your face." I rushed to the washroom to clean up.

In the lobby we found the clerk dead. His throat was slashed. Those jerks were sloppy. Anyone could see the body from the door as it lay between the counter and foyer. We made a hasty retreat. Once again we had nowhere to go and ever fewer provisions. We did take the clips from the automatic weapons which we tossed in the dumpster behind the hotel. Our walk last afternoon paid off as we used the park trails to stay hidden. Side streets didn't guarantee our cover. As we continued our journey, human forms emerged from the shadows. Needless to say we drew our firearms as they surrounded us. "Check out their eyes." Cloey glanced behind us. "They're all infected." "So I see." I answered. I counted fifteen heads before I gave up. All of them had weapons and no particular dress code. On the positive side, I saw no guns. Plenty of bats and steel bars though. Some had knives. Others, hatchets, axes and hammers. I singled out a young man ahead of the crowd. He brandished a samurai sword and a large scar across his cheek. "Must be their leader. Keep your gun low." I gave Cloey a soft nudge and she nodded. The large native stopped dead and raised his hand. When he balled it to a fist, the others stopped. In the street light I could see he'd shaved the left side of his head. It looked goofy. "Wrong place and time for an evening stroll. You're obviously not from around here . . ." One of his minions interrupted and whispered in his ear. When he was done, he stepped aside. The leader smirked. "You shot one of us, not wise. You know what that means?" I was tired, not from lack of sleep alone, but of this god forsaken town. The childish question-answer period did little more than perturb me further and I whispered to Cloey to prepare to flee. "No jackass, please enlighten me." The smirk faded. His pupils brightened. "You're both dead, that's what." The gang began to circle. If we didn't turn and burn we'd have no escape. "Now!" I barked. We wheeled around and raced full speed up the street and toward the nearest park. The tree cover would give us an advantage. Out in the open we were sitting ducks. It didn't take much brainstorming to realize who the 'one of us' I shot was. The stranger who wanted Cloey is who he referred to. Gang membership went deeper than race, age or gender. All one had to do was tap into Occuchip's insanity and zap, instant in. Good thing Cloey got out when she did or I'd really have been screwed. We headed into the park and for the first cluster of trees. We positioned ourselves for a good line of sight in case we had to blast our way out. I heard someone call for a torch and in seconds three flashlights combed the area.

"They're here somewhere." The unmistakable grunt of their chief echoed through the park. One light swept over us and we ducked. "Over here." Footsteps sounded like thunder as they neared. We'd been spotted and were pretty much cornered. We drew our guns and fired into the crowd. Two of the gang dropped and one threw a hammer. It missed Cloey's head by less than an inch and we again ducked behind the trees. Other projectiles flew over our heads. I assumed they were rocks. I squeezed Cloey's hand. She was shaking. We'd met our match and here we would die. It was inevitable.

From a distance the familiar pop of firecrackers filled the air. The gang began to shout at one another and in an instant they were running amok in a blind panic. The pop was not firecrackers, but the rain of bullets from automatic rifles. I peeked around the tree. Bodies dropped around us like flies. "What's going on?" Cloey asked as she peered over my shoulder. "I don't know." I answered. "Looks like the cavalry's coming." The one-sided firefight was over in minutes. When the ammo stopped flying and everyone but us was wounded or dead, we crept to the trail. We were about to head further into the park, away from our saviors. As much as we wanted to give thanks we didn't want to be next. We hadn't made it more than a few steps when a spotlight hit us. "If you want to live, I suggest you drop your weapons and turn around slowly." We couldn't see anyone through the glare and our pistols fell to the gravel. I kept my eyes closed to avoid the blinding light. I imagine Cloey did the same. "On your knees." The male voice directed. Gravel dug into my jeans and pressed sharply against my skin as I obeyed. Two men rushed over and cuffed us before dragging us to our feet. "Easy, you prick!" Cloey shouted. The flood light lowered and I took note that our captors wore camouflage fatigues. The one dealing with Cloey slapped the back of her head. "Shut up bitch." We were led from the park to awaiting squad cars. We weren't read any rights or asked any questions. Cloey was placed in the back of one car and me the other. These were not typical cops. They packed their hardware in the trunk. Their cars bore no insignia and were painted black. The inside was typical, with a cage in the back and a computer up front. Were these the head of Occuchip security? If so our flight was over. For now the near future was out of our hands.

What could've been twenty minutes or two hours trickled by. The ride lasted no more than ten and the rest was spent waiting in an interrogation room. Cloey must have been in another undergoing the same barrage of questions. "What's your name? What were you doing wandering the streets at night? Where are you from?" Just to name a few. I was also asked my mother and father's name. Though I answered honestly, I was bewildered by the interest. When they had the information they needed I was escorted down a hallway. As in my nightmares I was led to a holding cell. Unlike the dream, no arm came from the food slot and the man in a white coat wasn't with us. There was one other in the confined cinder block space, my beloved Cloey. I was shoved inside and the squeaky door slammed shut. I stepped over and perched beside her on the cold concrete bench. "Long time no see." She wrapped an arm around my waist and I followed suit. "No kidding," she said. "They question you about your life?" "You know it." I answered, "Except my sex life. What do you suppose they'll do with us?" She sighed, "I don't know, but it can't be good." I had to agree. She released me, stood and walked to the small glass window. "Have you noticed we seem to be the only ones here?" Her tone was low and serious. "What do they do in this town, kill the criminals?" "Who knows Cloe, you might not be far off. Don't suppose we're next, do you?" "I don't know **what** they're planning. It doesn't matter anyhow. They're gonna do what they want regardless." She was right but I couldn't see us coming this far for nothing. I didn't believe we would die. They wanted something from us, I just didn't know what. They'd make it clear soon enough. I hoped we weren't to be experimented on like in my dreams. The thought of that large needle made me cringe. I sprawled on the bench with my ideas of what could be while Cloey paced the floor. "How long do you suppose we've been here?" Cloey held her stomach. Mine ached as well. Sure we had plenty of water but no food. Weren't prisoners provided three meals a day? They must've been trying to break us. "Over twelve hours for sure." My head filled with reassuring phrases to soothe Cloey's restlessness but to speak them out loud would come off as girlish and lame. Instead I continued to lay with her. Though my hope for the best remained, it dwindled by the hour. I had to keep up a positive facade to keep from depressing us both.

    I woke up to Cloey shaking me. She said I'd slept approximately an hour. "Someone's coming, get up." So up I got. The footsteps reached our door and the guard that had brought Cloey in poked his face in the window. The food slot clicked open and in slid a tray with two plates of chicken, mashed potatoes and buttered bread. "Eat up." He said. "The captain'll be here within the hour. He wants a word with you two." Cloey brought the tray over to the bench. We were about to dig in to the generous portions when the guard tapped on the door. Two steaming Styrofoam cups sat on the ledge. I motioned Cloey to stay while I retrieved them. "Thank you." I told the guard before he closed the hatch. He mumbled, "Whatever" and headed off. A sweet aroma tantalized my smell receptors. "Hot chocolate." I gave Cloey hers and sat down to the meal. "Well, this is nice." I lifted the plastic fork to my mouth. I could taste the potatoes before they reached my tongue. "Not yet. We should give thanks." I set the fork down. Drool leaked through my lips and I wiped it away. We gave our thanks to the powers that be and dove into our food.

When we were done, we rinsed chicken grease from our fingers in the stainless steel sink. We used toilet paper to dry off with. After, we cuddled on the bench. We both fell asleep this time, but not for long. I was dreaming of home and how I wished to return. Rapidly the vision changed to Mister Morris' living room. I was tracing the blood trail to the bathroom . . . The grind of the hinges woke me. Our guards stood in the doorway. Cloey pushed herself up and rubbed her eyes. "Come along you two." Wearily I stood and stretched. Before long we were again sitting in an interrogation room. Our wrists were cuffed to the legs of a steel table bolted to the floor. Across from us with hands folded were our camouflage heroes. The way they stood reminded me of the security at Buckingham palace in London. An Austin Powers movie came to mind and I began to giggle at the way he made fun of them. Cloey told me to shush, which made things worse. I no longer tried to conceal my laughter. It didn't help anyway. My captor slammed his hand on the table and glared at me. The luminance reflecting settled me immediately. I wondered if everyone in the town was under Occuchip influence. "That'll be enough." Due to the cuffs I couldn't turn to see who was behind us, but the youthful pitch was well known. A flutter of excitement pulsed through my gut. "Danny, is that you?" He rounded the table. It was him alright. He was taller and unmistakably wiser. "Hey bro how's your eighth month of being on the run? You know I thought a lot about you while in that mental hospital. Where were you and why didn't you visit anymore? You had mom worried you know." "How **is** mom?" I asked. "Have you seen her lately?" Danny hid his emotions well. I couldn't tell if he was pleased or angry with me. I could only guess through his words. "She talked of you often and yeah, I see her now and then. She died last month. She's buried at the St. Peter cemetery. Look at you, so many miles from home. You know you've covered half of southern B.C.?" I couldn't speak. Mom was dead and I didn't even say goodbye. I lowered my head in shame. "Don't be too upset Ben. I told her I'd find you and take care of you and hey, why not? You took me under your wing for years, may as well return the favor. We'll start with the restraints." He snapped his fingers and the guards removed the cuffs and left the room. "I hope my men didn't treat you too poorly. Good thing we found you when we did. The Nihilists don't take prisoners. That's the gang you pissed off. It pays to know your turf after dark. And you miss," He sized up Cloey and grinned. "Miss Clover Riley, nice to finally meet you face to face. I've heard so much about you I feel as if we're family." "How?" Danny looked at me as if I were stupid. Perhaps to him I was. "You really didn't ask that, did you? Oh brother of mine, I can clearly see you're an Occuchip reject, but come on. Think about it. You're the one who let me try out the software after all." Of course, Danny was the prime example of how the program was meant to work. His chemistry and mindset were a perfect match, which made him one of the few to resist the infection. "Now you've got it and yes, I can read your thoughts. One thing you've got wrong. There's no infection. Addictive behavior is the cause of all the problems. You've seen drunks and junkies before. You know how it is when they stop using. They recover, don't they? And if they keep using they go insane or die. It's the nature of the beast Ben. Fortunately for you, you have an allergy of sorts. Your brain had a unique reaction and rejected most of the assimilated info. Clover's did as well but not nearly to the same extent. No wonder you two are so evenly matched. You know I've been tracking you for the last month? A real shame about your aunt Emma. I'm glad you shot the guy who killed her. He would've killed you too Ben, but you Clover? You he would've kept as his toy. He was evil, that one." "You must be linked with everyone who's used the system." Cloey stood and leaned on the table. "Why not us?" "He's already told us Cloe. We're not part of the system. We don't hold enough mega bytes or whatever they call it, am I right?" "Bingo." Danny chimed. "You're curious aren't you? Go ahead and ask what you want. I'll answer honestly." I had one question only. If Danny could run a section of town, how high was he in the pecking order? "How many are like you? What I mean is . . ." "I know what you mean," He cut in. "I'm the only one I know to completely accept the entire program. As far as my established position in society, let's put it this way, I rule this town. No one comes or goes without my knowledge, not even you. You did absorb one aspect of the system. You can be tracked. The first command of the program is to give you an individual signature unique to anyone else's. That is how I find you." Cloey sat down and whispered in my ear. Danny's eyes darted back and forth between us. He seemed confused. "The people who tried to rob us at our hotel didn't use computers. They weren't tagged. I could tell by their eyes." Danny sighed. "Yeah, well, not everyone is perfect. They're what we call the remnants of society. They'll be faded out soon enough. You'll be happy to know we put down the two you allowed to live. The hotel's being cleaned as we speak. It'll be open for business in a matter of hours. It's the last hotel to accept cash and we find many remnants rent there. Some we're able to work with. Others well, you know." I couldn't believe what I was hearing. My own brother was playing god. I began to resent helping him all these years. He wasn't who I knew him to be. The complete opposite is what he'd become and I blamed myself for accepting the damn package that day. Unknowingly I created a monster and damned this town and everyone who came near it. I slammed my first on the table and jumped up. "Come on Cloey, we're leaving." "Hold it." He called as we turned to go. "I haven't told you why you're here." "I know why we're here." Cloey snapped. Danny pursed his lips. He knew we were done playing his game. "You resent Ben for being smarter than you. You think by toying with us you'll finally have one up on him, but let me tell **you** pal, nothing you do to us will ever replace the fact that you're a cold-hearted heathen and will always be second best." He clenched his teeth and balled his fists. "Is that how you feel Ben? You gonna go with your harlots opinion over the love of your brother?" "I don't know," my calm poise bothered him. Cloey had shown me the chink in his armor the moment she whispered in my ear. I only needed to wait to see it for myself. "You tell me." He didn't know how I felt. The extent of his mind reading was hindered by my connection to Cloey. I could follow her and he'd kill us both or choose his path and watch her die. The decision was simple. Life without her wouldn't be worth living. I loved my brother more than he knew, but love had limits. No way would I follow him on his path to hell. No way. Danny whistled for his minions. They must have been standing right outside the door. The one who arrested me came in and blocked our exit. The other stood just outside. "Where do you think you're gonna go, huh? You have no weapons, no protection. I can give you everything you need, bro. I can give you the life you've given me." His eyes pleaded for my submission. I thought of the times when he needed me most, like when I'd stand up against kids that would belittle him and call him retarded. I recalled his innocent style and simple ways. A tear rolled down my cheek. Those things were gone forever. I gave the most open answer I had. "Thanks Danny, but we're not the same people anymore. I can't live the way you do. It's time to go our separate ways. No hard feelings." I held my hand out. Reluctantly he took it. He had the oddest expression. Not sad or spiteful, but barren as a desert landscape. "Okay, no hard feelings." He motioned to the guards and they backed off. "You're free to go." "That's it?" Cloey asked. "Yeah," he smirked. "That's it." Cloey started for the door, notably concerned. I trailed behind giving Danny one last long look before walking from the room. "Uh, just one more thing." We both turned around. His eyes, pupil, cornea and whites shone bright. I'd never seen the likes of it before or since. Cloey gasped in amazement. "Be careful out there. Lots of crazies, but you know that already." He shooed us away. I remember thinking his sarcastic arrogance would be his downfall. I can still hear him humming C.C.R.'s 'bad moon rising' as we left. It was his favorite tune.

"So where do we go from here?" We stood outside the police station. The sun was setting. Soon darkness would surround us and we'd be defenseless. I had to think quickly, though the one thing that came to mind wasn't relevant to our situation. Though Danny was three inches taller, he still dressed in scrubby tee shirts and jeans. His body and mind may have matured but not his fashion sense. In some ways he was still a child. Was it possible he could have killed mom while having a tantrum? He said nothing of dad. Perhaps he did to him what he had to the woman at the store. Dad might have taken her life in a rage Danny planted in his subconscious. It was a theory and of course there was no proof, though given Danny's disposition, it was plausible. So there I was searching for an answer to Cloey's query and coming up blank. "I really don't know." I said while observing the sun creep across the sky. Time was running out. "Find shelter and arm ourselves I guess." "What about supplies? We need food and water." I dug in my pockets. I still had nearly twenty-five dollars left. "Do you have any cash?" She rolled her eyes. "Not anymore. It was taken when we were, like everything else we need." "Okay," I sighed. "It looks like we'll be going shopping. Let's hope Danny boy didn't convert food outlets to credit or debit only." "And suppose he did, then what?" I took Cloey by the hand and we headed out. "Then my dear, we shoplift."

The first place we found was a corner store. We grabbed enough munchies for the night and next morning, which ate up the remains of my change. I got the idea to search the phone book for R.V. lots and found one on the other side of town. We were heading that way anyway, so we chanced it. With plastic bags in hand we began our long walk. My biggest concern was the sun staying up until we made it. We were still several blocks away when dusk settled in. I had the unnerving sensation we were being followed and I let Cloey know about it. "Me too." She kept checking over her shoulder. I asked her to stop. "Don't let them know we know. Listen for footsteps between traffic. We'll stop every block for a rest. We can do our surveillance then." And that is how it was until a block from our destination. Though we scoured our surroundings on every break, we could neither see nor hear anything to verify our fears. Still we stayed vigilant and dodged between the buildings until we made it. Security patrolled the parking lot. We were able to avoid being seen by staying in between the trailers and keeping low. Cloey would let me know when it was safe to try one of the trailer doors. The first four units were locked. I assumed they all were and decided to break into the next one. It was easy. The windows didn't slide and the vent was open partially. I reached my fingers in and popped the safety catch, which opened it outward as an emergency exit. We timed the guard so we knew he was out of sight and I boosted Cloey in. She came around back and unlatched the door. "That wasn't so difficult was it?" I asked once we were secure in our temporary home. "Not too shabby," she agreed. She kissed my cheek. "Oh Damn, I left the groceries outside. I'll be right back." I rushed out before security returned. If they spotted our stuff we'd be done for. I was heading toward the rear of the trailer when a black sedan flew carelessly into the parking lot. Its high beams washed over me as it turned toward the main office. They didn't see me, thank heaven and I hurried inside. "There you are. I see . . ." I held my finger to my lips and shuffled Cloey to the bedroom. "It looks like we were followed after all. Stay low. I'll check things out." I scurried to the window I'd helped Cloey through. I knelt on the bench below it and made sure it was locked. I drew the curtains enough that I could still see out and waited for movement. Before long a flashlight beam swept across the lot. Two men came into sight. One was the security guard. The other I recognized immediately. It was the soldier who arrested Cloey. "Damn!" I spat under my breath. He was carrying a handgun. He cocked the slide and motioned for the guard to follow. They searched between trailers, being sure to check underneath each one. Through the silence I heard their dialogue. "Are they usually locked?" The soldier asked as he moved toward us. He tried the doors on two of the units. "I'll check a couple more if you don't mind." There was one other trailer in the row that he hadn't checked besides ours. I left the window and crawled to the door. I was positive I hadn't latched it. The soldier told mister security to keep an eye out. He would check one more door before he left. If anyone was seen in the area he was to be notified immediately. As I reached for the dead bolt his hand fell on the knob. I clenched my teeth and prayed he wouldn't hear the click or open the door before the bolt locked into place. The door shook as he yanked on it. It stayed shut. I let out a low sigh of relief, and then held my breath until his footfalls faded. When all was quiet, I crawled over to Cloey and cuddled with her on the bed. "Are you hungry?" She asked after several minutes. I was a little. I didn't want to eat. I'd be more agile and alert on an empty stomach. We may have late night visitors yet.

Night gave way to a cloudy sky. Though I hadn't slept more than a few winks at a time, Cloey had. When she raised her head she commented on my choice to sit in the walkway, rather than on the bed with her. I let her know it was the best way to avoid sleep. "You just wanted to protect me didn't you, my guardian angel." She kissed my forehead. "We should leave before this place opens," I suggested. "We can find a quiet area to eat on our way out of town." She recommended staying close to the highway so we could hitch a ride. "What'll we do for a weapon?" I didn't want another episode like our previous encounter. "We'll fight together if there's any danger. We will be the weapons." I agreed with her. Two heads were better than one after all. I still would've felt better with a blunt instrument or knife.

In a wooded area off the highway we had lunch. My arms were weak and sore from the weight of the bags. Cloey offered to help carry them but I refused her. I told her it was what gentlemen do and she complimented the way my parents raised me. "It's good to see chivalry's not dead." I told her it was common decency. She hugged me and I passed her the cookies. She loved chocolate chip as much as I. Traffic blew by as though nothing had changed. How long would it take before every road was littered with dead cars and bodies? It would depend on how rapidly the virus spread, and there were millions of computers out there. Many would no doubt receive the infamous package in the mail and curiosity would drive them to use it. How easy to be thankful for the little things when uncertainty loomed with every move we made. Despite the danger, we both smiled. When every second counted it was pointless to dismiss the calm in expectation of the storm. The warmth of the mid summer air and coolness of the grass under us provided a sense of safety. I must have fallen asleep. When I awoke Cloey prompted me to get going. I asked how long I'd been out and she told me at least two hours. I knew then I should've taken in a few hours the night before. Despite my grogginess we made our way down an embankment to the steady stream of traffic. "Keep an eye out for black sedans. We don't want to be caught off guard." Cloey nodded. "We should also watch who we ride with. Nobody large enough to take us both on. Women and elderly preferably." I agreed. We passed a sign that read Highway One. We were heading toward Vancouver on the west coast. That meant since my journey began so many months ago I'd been traveling in a zig zag. I still had no clue as to where we were. The city's name would be with me until I left it. Cloey had the same problem. She called it a fail safe created to keep rebellious minds on a tether. Though inconvenient, it hadn't counted on our united strong will. If it wanted to dissuade us or shorten the leash it would have to try harder. I wondered why it wouldn't erase our minds and get it over with. It could start again and we wouldn't be the wiser. Perhaps it couldn't because of our will to survive. Determination to become better than we were could be the answer. Not better physically or mentally, but spiritually. A burning desire for goodness and hope for all instead of selfish gain was our safety net. That would explain why Danny held his strong position and we had nothing. We were outcast and hunted simply because we wouldn't conform to ways that threatened our individuality. I could no longer consider Danny my brother because of it, but at least I had a new companion. Cloey held her thumb out and walked backward. The odd car would slow but none stopped. Not until we tread a kilometer or more. Finally a grey Toyota pulled ahead of us. We jogged over and were pleased to see an elderly lady. She wore thick round glasses. If she gave us any trouble we could knock them off her face and blind her long enough to subdue her. Things must be bad for me to consider restraining an old person. Regardless it was how it was and we wouldn't be fooled again. I climbed in through the rear passenger door and allowed Cloey the front. She greeted us with a wry grin. She gave us her name and offered us a cigarette. When we declined she perked up. "I don't smoke either. My son's wife left them on the seat a week back. I call her my son's wife because I got no use for her as a daughter-in-law. Bad news she is, dragging him to bars and dance clubs. I don't know what he sees in her. Hmm, must be her intelligence. You know just cuz yer knowledgeable, doesn't mean yer smart. You look like a couple of bright kids. Heading home or away from?" I gave Cloey the floor. The women could talk while I rested. "A little of both I suppose. We're getting married soon and we're searching for a suitable town to settle into." "Married huh?" She must've thrown it out for good measure. "Well I hope you steered clear of . . ." She named the city we just left. Sorry I can't remember the name. "That place is a dive. The law that runs it is more corrupt than any place I've been. They've got this policy that you can't stay overnight if you have no immediate family there. Silly huh? They claim to be an upgraded computerized unit or such. I don't have much use for any world outside the one I was born into, so I don't have any computer knowledge. I guess they i.d. you by password. What kind of world do we live in when a community can reject you for being yourself? A greedy one that goes against basic

*VISIONS*

Christian principals is what. You seem like God fearing people. You ain't J.W.'s are you?" "No, ma'am, we don't go by any religion. I like to call ourselves spiritual." She was doing great, keeping personal information far from the conversation. "Yer not those hippie types are you? You know the kind who smoke flowers and sing about serenity and sex? Well, if y'are, don't be preachin' to me. I went through that phase years ago. Never did take part in it, but sure had to hose a few of ya off my lawn. Back in the sixties yer kind was everywhere. If you weren't a soldier you'd be camped out wherever ya figured you had to spread love and my lawn was no baby makin' camp." "You must have the wrong idea ma'am. We're nothing of the sort. We don't do drugs. If I didn't know any better I'd say you lived in the states." "Well young lady, I sure did. California to be exact. We had our own orange tree right out front our living room window. The biggest pests it attracted were them hippies. My husband and I moved up here way back when. He got himself a job with the railroad. He died a couple winters ago." "I'm sorry to hear that." I said, breaking my silent streak. She looked at me through the rearview. "**I'm** not. He had cancer. He had a good life with little regret. Best he died when he did. Saved him a lot of pain. He was hit by a truck while crossing our street. Died instantly instead of having his body rot out from the inside. I'd say he was most fortunate. By the way, you didn't say your names." "I'm Sven and this is Becca." Cloey gave me one of those 'are you kidding me' frowns. The kind where her lips were twisted and her stare said 'idiot'. She rolled her eyes and turned to the windshield. "Well it was good talking with you." She slowed the car. We weren't at the exit yet and my adrenaline pumped. I hope Cloey was watching for a weapon. "There's a dirt path up that way that'll lead you to a good place." She said as she pulled to a stop. "Good luck with you." We climbed out and she pulled away. Cloey spotted the trail and we headed for it. "Really Ben, Becca and Sven? Do I look like a Becca to you?" "Sorta." I answered. "Okay Swedish meatball, you can carry my bag." She shoved the neatly tied bundle of snacks and water into my stomach. "It's common courtesy, chivalry man."

We hiked for what felt like an hour before we reached a clearing and chose to rest. Cloey and I were confused and disoriented. We looked at each other and knew we had the same thing on our minds. It was Cloey who broke the silence. "Where the hell are we going? It's like we've been walking in circles." I dropped to the soft grassy earth and clasped my hands behind my head. As I lay there with no solution, Cloey picked up our supply bag. She opened it and helped herself to some water. "You don't think the ol' girl led us astray, do you?" I asked as I beckoned for a drink. She passed me the bottle, set the bag down and sat across from me. "I don't know," she said as I took a swallow. "We can't be too far from civilization. What should we do?" When I was young, my father told me if I couldn't decide my next plan of action, I should stay put until the answer came. 'Listen to the voice inside you.' He used to say. 'It will always steer you right.' It was sound advice that I don't recall having to follow. Well, here was an opportunity. "We'll rest until either of us can come up with something, okay?" She agreed and we lay together. As we stared off into the clouds I heard the snap of a branch and knew we'd been found. By who wasn't clear, but being found when we weren't lost boosted our tracker to enemy status. Cloey and I scrambled to our feet and a young couple dressed in fatigues emerged from the bushes. I grabbed the food and prepared to bolt. "Don't be alarmed." The woman said as she stepped forward. She had a pleasant smile. Blonde hair protruded from beneath her cap. She couldn't have been more than nineteen. I guessed the male to be her boyfriend as he too stepped from the foliage. He also wore a camouflage cap and didn't appear much older. "What are you two running from?" He demanded. I scowled and spat. "Who says we're running and why are **you** concerned?" He glared at me before studying Cloey. She was focused at the gun holstered to his side. I hadn't seen it until then. "Relax." The girl encouraged. "We're on the same side. You must be familiar with . . ." "Quiet, Jen." The guy snarled. "We don't know these two. They could be linked." It was obvious by 'linked' he meant to the Occuchip system. There was no glow from either set of eyes and I had the distinct belief they were what Danny called remnants. I ventured out by exposing a piece of ourselves. Cloey looked at me in disbelief but said nothing. She understood enough to know I wouldn't put us in harms way. "Does Occuchip mean anything to you two? It does to us. Now drop your superiority complex so we can talk. Trust has to start somewhere." The two glanced to each other, then to us. "Come on." The guy said as he turned. "Follow us, we'll go somewhere safe. If you can find us, so can others." They guided us through the bush, steering clear of the trails. We were warned to tread carefully as to not carve a path and I became distracted by my diligence. Before I knew it, we we're standing inside a small camp with an army green tent for shelter. Four logs were set as benches around a fire pit. No fire was burning and by the looks of it, had never been. They must've set up recently. The guy beckoned us to sit before asking our names. Much to

Cloey's disapproval I used our other names. "I'm Kirk and this is Jen. As you may have noticed we don't like crowds. We've been traveling through these woods for over a week now. The city life has gotten too crazy for us." "Tell me about it." I concurred. "Becca and I have been well educated there . . ." I continued on with my experiences after leaving home and the developments that prompted me to do so. When I reached the part where I met Cloey, I stopped. "So you know of the disease being spread through computers?" Jen was nervous. The way she clung to Kirk caused me to believe there was more to her story then she was letting on. I was about to find out exactly what it was. "Sure we know." Cloey said as she nudged me with her elbow. "If it wasn't for the virus, we'd never have met." "Only it isn't a virus." I cut in. I was compelled to set the record straight. "It's much more, like a consciousness with selfish intent. It seems when the user doesn't accept full programming, or rather when it doesn't get its way, it throws a tantrum. Basically it forces whoever is affected by it to do its bidding or suffer." "Like it did to my mom," Jen wiped a tear from her cheek. "Our stories are similar. Before Kirk and I met up, I lived in Penticton . . ." Penticton? The name was familiar to me. "My mom had gone to a corner store for a few groceries. I wasn't home when she returned because a friend invited me to spend the night. The next day, I found out she'd killed my dad and younger brother and sister before killing herself. I wasn't mentioned in the paper as being a family member. It was like I never existed. I thought it was because my dad was my step dad and not blood related, but then my friends began to treat me like they didn't know who I was. I couldn't go home so I left town and came out this way. I met Kirk at the same time. That was more than half a year ago." "Yeah," I said, "Closer to nine months." Jen removed her cap and brushed away the hair that fell over her face. She looked at me with a stern curiosity that beckoned for more information. Her query confirmed. "How do **you** know? Did you read about it in the paper? It wasn't published outside of town so you must have been there." Finally I had confirmation of where I'd come from and this time the name stuck. I was from Penticton, wherever it was. My good ol' brother and I were unfortunate enough to meet up with Jen's mom and I suddenly felt guilty for destroying her life. My palms were perspiring and a cold emptiness swept through my soul. What was the purpose for us coming together like this? Was I being punished for dabbling in the Occuchip world, or was it merely a coincidence and my imagination had labeled me condemned? I didn't believe in coincidences so that left one opening. I had by my own decision ruined Jen's future. How many others? I didn't belong here. Sooner or later Cloey would be brought down by me as well. I stood. My hand trembled. "I . . . I have to go. I can't be here. You're not safe." "Wait." Jen demanded. "What is it you're not telling us?" "Nothing." I stammered. My mind went hazy. All I could recall is bolting through the brush. Voices shouted after me. I stumbled. When I tried to push myself up I was pinned down. I remember being rolled onto my back and staring into Kirk's angry glare. Cloey knelt beside me. I gasped heavily for air. "My god, look at his eyes!" I heard Jen squeal. My breathing changed to dangerously shallow when her shriek permeated my ears. My head and chest ached and my blood ran cold. I was sure my heart would stop. The kaleidoscope effect hindered my vision. I was having a mental lapse. "Hold her." Kirk instructed Jen. "If he's one of them then she might be too."

We were found out. We weren't remnants or infected, we were somewhere in the middle which made everyone our foes. A jolt of searing agony tore through my body and rested in my head. The last thing I heard before blacking out was my own scream.

We were back in the camp when I came to. Cloey and I were tied to separate trees a few feet apart. My head weighed a ton and a rag that had been shoved in my mouth prevented me from calling to her. She had been beaten by the looks of it, and quite badly. Her face was heavily bruised and blood streaks ran from her nose down her chin. How she held her head up was a mystery. Kirk noticed I was up. He set the stick down that he was prodding the fire with and sauntered over. Jen popped her head out of the tent. "Don't hurt them anymore." She begged. "Mind your business." He barked back. She rushed over to join us. "At least let him tell us what we want to know. We could be wrong about them. The girl didn't lie. She told us their names. I don't know why you had to beat her like that." "Shut up. We don't know anything. They've lied to us once. Let's just hear what he has to say and I'll decide then if I can trust him." He lifted my chin and pulled the gag from my mouth. Though my lids fought to close I forced them open. "Tell me your name, your real name." There was no need to hide my identity nor for any more questions. I know what they were after and gladly gave it. "Ben Wilson. I'm from Penticton." "Wait a minute. Jen, grab us a seat. We're gonna be here a while." Jen came from the tent with two folding chairs. I hoped one was for me. The rope was digging into my wrists and rubbing them raw. To my dismay, Kirk and Jen sat on them and Kirk asked, "You don't by chance have a brother by the name of Danny, do you?" I nodded. I didn't wish to be labeled with him but I didn't want to lie either. "Son of a bitch, I told you he's one of 'em." I didn't know how Danny had affected him, only that it wasn't good. The backhand to the jaw confirmed it. "Enough, Kirk, let him continue." "It's my fault." I said. "My brother was mentally slow and the label said the program could improve mental abilities. I only wanted to help. It backfired. I tried the software first, but only once. I thought it was some kind of game so I let Danny try it. I cut him off when he showed signs of addiction. Somehow, it affected him differently. He was the reason your mom did what she did, Jen. We were at the store at the same time. All he did was look at her and I saw the flash of light. She changed right then. I'm sorry." Jen put her hands to her mouth. "Oh, my god." "I swear I'm not one of them. I don't wish to harm anyone. My brother has people hunting us. Please, let us go and we'll leave. We'll never bother you again." Kirks lip curled. "Alright. You can leave. Jen, untie the girl." She smiled and went to Cloey. Through the bruises, concern and uncertainty showed. She said nothing as Jen released her bonds but I knew she doubted Kirk's intentions. He freed my hands and I was able to push myself up. I rubbed my wrists and waited for instruction. Cloey rushed over and latched on. She buried her head in my chest and I stroked her hair. "Oh, isn't that sweet." Kirk mocked. We turned and faced him. "You said we could go." Cloey's throat was raspy. "Give us our supplies and we'll leave." "Sorry, that's not part of the deal." Jen intervened. "What are you doing Kirk? You're not sending them away empty handed." "Shut up Jen," he snapped. "**I'm** in charge. Besides, we need to eat too. Now get out of here. Spread your plague elsewhere." Jen stormed over to Kirk. She had apparently had enough of his bullying. "Give them water at least, or I'm leaving with them." He bared his teeth and shoved her. She stumbled back and fell on her ass. "You bastard!" She screamed. "What's gotten into you?" "I said shut up!" By that time I'd had enough. I told Cloey to stay and marched up to Kirk. Before I reached him he drew his pistol and shoved it in my face. "Not a good time to play hero kid, now turn around and walk away or I will shoot you both." Normally I would've raised my hands in a defensive gesture, but I was too irate. I kept them at my sides. "Alright, were going. Come on Cloe, we'll find somewhere else." I wrapped my arm around her waist. "I know." She said. "We always do." I took one final glance behind us. Jen was on her feet. I heard a click before I could fully turn around and that's when life went to slow motion. Before the shot rang out I was able to push Cloey away and yell 'down'. The 'pop' of the weapon reverberated all around and I dove for cover. Another shot rang out, but not from Kirk's gun. It came from the direction we we're heading. When I looked up I heard Kirk shout in pain. His body crumpled to the earth. I crawled to Cloey. "Someone's firing at us. Kirks been hit." "Me too," she moaned and rolled to her side. "Where, I don't see." "My right side, it's burning." I still couldn't see the injury and didn't have time to examine her further. Maybe she injured herself when she fell. "Stay here, I'll be back in a sec." I left her and crawled toward Kirk. Jen lay beside him. "Toss me the gun." I prompted. "No" she countered. "Stay away, keep low." Voices echoed through the trees. Danny's minions had found us. There was no more time. I spotted Kirk's gun in the grass a few feet away. I was closer to it then Jen. I scrambled up and grabbed it. Two figures came into view. I hoped they wouldn't spot me as I crawled back to Cloey. Jen shrieked and I snapped my head her way. She stood and turned to run but a projectile found the base of her skull and she dropped. Cloey called me. Her plea came in a shallow gasp. She was lying on her back when I reached her. Blood saturated her shirt and stained the ground beneath. She had been hit after all. "Run." She beckoned. "Save yourself." I didn't want to leave her. My mind raced with every excuse to stay by her side, but before I could use any, the soft glow shone once more in her pupils. "It's okay." She didn't speak it. We were telepathically linked. "Go, I'll always be with you." A warm smile graced her lips. "I love you." I knew I had to leave. Her smile didn't fade as I backed away. I made my way through a group of ferns and lay still. The two men entered the camp. One went over to Jen and Kirk. He searched the ground and I knew he was looking for the gun. If only he knew I had it trained on him. For the moment he was of no consequence, so I focused on the other. He towered over Cloey with his pistol in hand. He said something to her and she mouthed something in return. He raised the gun to her head and squeezed the trigger. A flood of emotion tore at my heart. All the anger and frustration I'd been avoiding washed over me. Accompanying it was unadulterated rage. I held nothing back as I jumped to my feet and squeezed off two rounds. The soldier who murdered my girl whirled around as the first bullet lodged in his shoulder. The second caught him square in his left eye. When his knees buckled I turned to the other. His pistol was strapped in the holster and he was fighting to draw it. "Send this message to my brother!" I shouted before unloading the final four rounds into his chest. His eyes lit up like high beams and I knew my discourse had been sent. I could envision Danny throwing a tantrum and cursing my name. I stomped over to my victim. I wanted to scream out my hatred at him, to send one final message to back off or else, to Danny. I said nothing as I hovered above. He stared up in disbelief and tried to raise his head. His hands were covered in blood and trembled as he held them over his stomach. The light faded from within, along with his final breath. I tossed Kirk's gun into the bushes and stripped off my rival's gun belt. I strapped it to my own waist and went over to Cloey. Kneeling beside her, I brushed tangled strands of hair off her face. A bullet hole marked the center of her forehead. I sat down and hoisted her to my lap. As I hugged her close, my emotion turned to deep sorrow and I balled like a child over the loss of my first and only love.

# Alone

Days went by and I staggered from place to place in search of food and water. Life no longer held any enjoyment. It was now simply a matter of how long I would survive. My brother was still out there and no doubt using painstaking effort to find me. I no longer cared. I avoided everyone. I had become that stray dog with no direction or real purpose, bound to live a life of solitude. The consciousness continued to spread. The country was in chaos. Murder had become a way of life and martial law had been declared across Canada. Anyone seen on the streets after dark would be shot and if they had no identification or were classed as a remnant that chose not to reform, they'd be tortured or imprisoned. Days stretched into months. How I made it this long was beyond me, but I took every precaution I could to remain undetected. Cloey's consciousness mixed with my own. Sometimes I could hear her guide me in my decision making. Every day she would tell me she loved me and encourage me to keep on going, despite my despair. Most nights I'd cry myself to sleep and she'd make her presence known. She'd assure me how special I was and prompt me to cling to what little hope I had. I knew we would meet again in another life and share eternity together. Strange as it may seem, I'm sure it was her idea for me to write these memoirs. I was conducted to catalogue our journey so the world may someday learn from us and avoid similar mistakes. For now I'm forced to inhale the heavy city air that bears the stench of garbage, gun power and exhaust. In the past week or so the sky has been clouded by the smoke of burning buildings and automobiles. Hell cometh quickly.

Anyhow, as I said when I began this story, I am perched behind a computer in the basement of a residence recently abandoned. My hearing has greatly improved. No telling when this house will hit the burn list or become overrun by locals. Less than half an hour ago I heard scratching noises around the front door. I checked it out and found nothing to verify my phobia. A small animal I guessed. Cat or raccoon, it probably smelled my ham sandwich and took off when it heard me coming. I have to get up and check my perimeter. I'll get back to the story in a moment, after a sweep of the place . . .

I've been noticing unusual sounds again. They've been going on for several minutes but are gaining intensity. I can no longer ignore them. Wait, I'm picking up voices. Oh no, I think they've found me. Yes, someone's here, hold

# ONE THOUGHT

by Steve Jennex

"Damn reception!" The old man must have been on the roof again, staggering in a drunken stupor. No doubt the skid row bastard had used the antenna for balance.

"Get off my roof!" The beer bottle in his hand shattered on the steel rail leading down the three steps to the sidewalk. Dad was searching, tracking the vagrant who interrupted his T.V. Show. Donald Faven held still, cowering beneath the woven wool cover his mother had made so long ago. It was his only material reminder of her. She must be in heaven. Dad said there was no such place, yet he himself had seen it many times through his dreams. Hell was real too. This life was proof enough. "There you are! Don't make me come up there." Footfalls above the two-room shack hastened, then stopped above his head. Soft scraping echoed through the thin concrete and proceeded down the wall. It ended with a soft 'thump' and quick 'oooh' as dad's adversary landed on the lawn. He could see the old man in his mind, shrouded in a grey torn jacket. A long matching beard and filthy old cowboy hat hid his features well. He was gathering his hat before jogging toward the street. Dad hadn't seen him, yet knew he was gone. Donald squeezed his eyes shut. Dad was rounding the house, broken bottle neck clutched in his right hand. Blood from his fingers dripped to the walkway. He was on his way in! There was nowhere to run and he would be blamed for allowing the man on the roof, another example of dad's insanity. He scanned the room for a place to hide. There was none. The windows had been barred ages ago and there was no bed to take solace under. A tattered foam mattress over the concrete floor was his bed, and his bathroom was nothing more than a steel bucket in the corner. Three years he'd been imprisoned in this confined space, never to be permitted outside the cell. As malnourished and pale as he was, his gaunt appearance may have shaken him had he a mirror to gaze into. No glass permitted, or he may have used a jagged shard to do himself in. A day and a half now he hadn't eaten, while his so-called caretaker pigged out on pizza, chicken and booze. Even then he was fortunate to receive scraps. Crusts and bones not fit for a dog was all he was worth . . . "Easy," he cautioned himself. He must relax and seek out his safe place. He could not allow it to escape again. Not after what happened to mother. It had been his fault, all his doing . . . He could hear dad digging in the fridge for another cold one. Once drank his torment would be relived. At ten years of age he couldn't comprehend the reason he was chosen for such severe and senseless beatings. Dad's rage brought down upon the child who killed his wife. "I'm sorry . . ." The sullen whisper replayed in his jumbled mind. 'I'm sorry, sorry . . .' Had the accident been his fault and his imagination the cause? He was angry then for not being permitted to swim in the neighbour's pool. "I hate you," he muttered at her under his breath, seconds before the

*VISIONS*

energy leapt from him. He intended to knock her to her knees on the deck. Instead she cracked her head on the side of the diving board before flopping into the water. By then sorry meant nothing, for she was dead before the splash. He knew because the power whispered 'It's over' as she fell. Dad's footfalls shook him from his thoughts. He had a new challenge. Don't cry. For every tear dad would beat him prior to the other abuse. Fear ripped through him, driving tears down his cheeks. 'Not again' he hoped. His insides still ached from the so-called quality time dad spent with him yesterday. Quality time? Torture, plain and simple. The beatings were far less painful. It had to stop, but no. He would not allow any bad ideas to surface, though prompted by the power for a change of heart. In the other room, beer bottles clinked against each other. Though he hadn't been allowed in there since the day he and dad moved, he vividly envisioned the layout. The coffee table had chips missing on every edge. Grease, dirt and beer stains coated glass fragments and crumbs. Surrounding them were empty cans and bottles that once held the elixir that drove dad to rage. "Son of a BITCH!" He was coming. "I tol' you keep yer damn friends away. Now yer gettin' it!" Frantically he sought cover and as usual, there was none. 'Stop him,' the power urged. It crept into his head and filled him with bitter courage. Too late to hold back now. Blood pumped forcibly behind his eyes. With lips pursed he allowed the power to seep from him. Dad tried the door. The knob wouldn't turn. With no lock it should have easily pulled open. "Open up or so help you . . ." It was building stronger than before. 'He deserves it.' As dad pounded on the door the protective force slammed into it, tearing it from its hinges and hurling it down the hallway. Dad stayed with it until it slammed him into the far wall. The boy stood with arms crossed and focused on the table with the beer cans and bottles. The man who never behaved like a father hit the floor with a dull thud. He was uninjured and tossed the door aside before scrambling to his feet. "Spawn of Satan," he bellowed. "I'll tear you a new ass!" Donald stepped forward and dropped his arms. No longer his frightened self, he shuffled into the foreign room. It was exactly as he pictured it, every detail crystal clear as in his imagination. A dangerous grin unfurled. Dad caught sight of it and his anger retreated. **He** was the fearful one now. "St . . . stay away!" He stumbled back, bounced off the edge of the table and flopped on his stomach beside the couch. Once bright blue, it bore stains from dirty hands and neglect. No different than the carpet and walls. One bottle vibrated and the top shattered, revealing jagged ridges below the cap line. Dad was on his knees. 'Justice.' The bottle swiftly jumped from the table and flew toward Donald. Mere inches from his face, it stopped and hovered. The broken end pointed his direction. What came next had been planned long ago, yet fear prevented it. No more. In that instant it rotated until the spout aimed away. Stale beer dripped to the floor before it hurled like a projectile toward the enemy.

Daylight approached as emergency vehicles arrived. On the sidewalk, Donald stood with a grey blanket draping his shoulders. Twilight slowly brightened to another cloudless day. Calm and pleased, he stared toward the shack as dad was removed. The bloody sheet revealed extensive damage to the flesh over his abdomen. "Turn away son," the officer suggested. He wouldn't. The cop strolled to his comrade. They attempted to hide their findings from him but were unable. He read their thoughts before they spoke. "Looks like a massacre in there. I've never seen anything like it. He may as well have had a grenade go off in his ass." "The coroner will have a challenge solving this. Any sign of intruders?" He glanced back to the house bordered with crime scene tape. "We found no prints other than of course, the boys and his fathers. It looks like he abused the poor kid. From what I saw he's been sleeping pretty much on the floor and crapping in a pail. If you ask me, the ass got what he deserved, no pun intended. Let's get him checked out at the hospital. No telling what else was done to 'em." The first officer scratched his temple. "I'll stay with him 'til we get there." He changed position to eye up the boy and asked, "Social Services been contacted?" "They'll meet you there. In the mean time forensics will have a tour. Maybe they can make sense of this." Donald wasn't about to be probed. The power could return and they would know he was involved. He would escape by closing his eyes and wishing for it. He could be anywhere he wanted by believing he was invisible. Not like before where he was bound by fear. With the power he would be free and away from doctors and social workers, to a place of his choosing. He **was** invisible . . . He opened his eyes. The town he'd grown up in was far away, replaced by a quiet rest area in the middle of nowhere. A road lay several feet ahead of him and to the far right, a small lake rippled in the light breeze. The scent of cooked meat wafted into his nostrils and he turned his head to follow it. A hotdog stand was propped on the far side of the gravel shoulder. A white and red umbrella shaded the hefty vender. Instantly his tummy growled. "For you. Eat." The power would feed him from now on. It was his new caretaker.

"Pull in here." The camper van bounced over the gravel rest stop. "Are we lost again?" The woman pestered as her husband huffed. "Come on hon, I know how to read a map." The facetious remark was ignored as he drove the van toward the hotdog stand. Donald eyeballed the vehicle until it came to a stop. The blanket the police gave him dropped from his shoulders. With bare feet he cautiously trod through the gravel, watching the ground for any sharp objects. These people could tell him his location. After, he would move on to find shelter. The couple climbed from the sliding side door and took each other's hand. They strolled over to the vender. Both looked to be in their late sixties or early seventies. He guessed them to be retired and on vacation, for the man's hands and face showed years of hard labor, as though he'd toiled under the sun much of his life. A farmer or construction worker he must have been. He made his way to them knowing they'd provide him with the food and information he sought. As he approached, the power stopped him in his tracks. 'They won't love you.' Of course not. That's why he kept isolated. But in need, keeping distant wasn't warranted. He ignored the voice and quickened his pace. "I'm lost." He told the vendor who dismissed him as he worked. The woman addressed him while her husband paid for the steaming franks. "Could you tell me where I am?" "My lord child," her concern startled him. Suppose she hurt him or lied like mom and dad? Would his anger be the source of **their** demise? "You look like you haven't eaten in a week. Honey, buy two more. This young man must be starving." She studied him with a puzzled expression. No shoes or shirt, only gym shorts. Where could he have come from? She extended a friendly hand and he rejected it by crossing his arms. Uncertain she let it fall to her side.

"I'm Carol." She glanced over to her husband who was collecting the hot dogs. "That's my husband Kevin. If you like you can eat with us at the camper." Though the kindness was appreciated, his plea still remained ignored. "I don't know where I am. I need to know." "Well," she began as she lowered to her haunches. "We're at a rest stop between Kamloops and Vernon. We just came through Falkland. We're on our way to Kelowna. If you have a phone number we could call your parents and perhaps they could meet us somewhere." He shook his head. The mere mention of his parents fueled his frustration. "No, I'll walk after I eat." "Walk?" Her condescending tone only angered him more. "We'll drive you." "No!" He felt cornered. The power began to seep from him. He would not allow it. These people didn't deserve it, so he would have to leave immediately after eating. "If you don't mind, I'll find my own way, but please, I'm so hungry." The woman called Carol frowned shrugged and beckoned him to the van. Kevin, who was not much of a talker, passed her the food and entered through the sliding door. After some shuffling he returned with two folding chairs. "Take a load off." He offered as he opened and propped them. Donald shook his head. The man shrugged and he and his wife took their seats. She handed him two hotdogs and he wolfed them down. When finished, he abruptly thanked the couple and turned to leave. "You sure you'll be alright?" Of course she'd be concerned about a young boy traveling alone, but she had no idea who he was. No clue just how well he could take care of himself. She would of course, inform the authorities when he was far enough away. It was time again to find a safe place. He would create his own using inspiration to take him where he wished to be. He closed his eyes and pictured a city. A place described long ago by a classmate. His buddy had grown up there. Abbotsford would be far enough away from the concrete shack and the memories of mom's untimely demise. 'They must not remember,' the power reminded. They wouldn't. Once out of sight they'd forget all about him.

"Where's the kid?" The two officers searched the perimeter of the shack, including the roof. He was gone. "He couldn't have vanished into thin air. I hope you took a photo of him." The second officer sheepishly stared at his shoes. In his camera were shots of the bedroom and the sandwich wrappers that littered the floor. The crime scene in the front room, along with the mess surrounding the body had been captured as well, which was why he had no snap shot of the boy. "I was about to. Unfortunately I forgot. In the excitement, I lost track." The first officer was thin yet muscular. He also had a tendency to lose his cool when confronted by stupidity. "Give me your sidearm." As he gestured for it, his confused partner asked why. "Never mind. Pass it or be suspended." An icy glare prompted obedience. Once in hand he raised it to his associate's chest. "Did you fail to reload as well?" "Of course not. Relax, you've made you point." His voice trembled. The safety clicked off. "I'd better check, can't be too cautious." Slowly he squeezed the trigger. "What are you doing? Are you crazy?" A satisfied smirk graced the cop's lips. He replaced the safety and released the clip. It fell to his palm. "Well, well, looky here. It's loaded after all." He returned the pistol then the clip. "Careful, there's one in the chamber. Don't forget again." He wheeled around and headed for his squad car. The second officer sighed with relief and with shaky hands, injected the clip. "Oh, Jeez." On wobbly legs he returned to his car and opened the door. Before climbing in he glanced to the wet patch on his slacks, his reminder of the importance of diligence on the job. "Oh, Jeez." He repeated.

Already in another city. How easy it was to transport with a simple desire. Alone again, he determined it best to stay that way. How tiring it was to be influenced by others and how good it felt to have no one concern themselves over his well being. It was time to seek shelter. Anywhere would be better than his previous prison. Somewhere inside a soft voice prompted him to find someone who could help. It wasn't the power, but a female plea which begged him to search for a loving home and to forgive himself. "No mother, I can't," he whispered. "My fault . . ." Depression overwhelmed him. Why would mother care for his soul after what he'd done? How could he redeem himself of his deficiencies? His consciousness and body were drifting through the rift as he sought a quiet place. In no time he'd arrived at a filthy pond in the heart of the city. He knew it as Mill Lake. He gazed into the murky water. From what he was told, it was a home to many cat fish and trout. An old train lined the bottom after plunging to the depths. That was many years ago and all that remained of the old mill were several log footings, which poked up from the water around the lake's edge. This was not an ideal spot. A green pasture embellished with a crystal clear brook would be more appropriate. No, not a standard green lawn, but a plush purple one under a florescent pink sky. No place existed but in his vivid imagination. Could it be possible for the power to take him there? Could it create a world of his choosing? 'All yours.' Yes, he understood it could be done. Anywhere he wished to be, there he'd arrive, but another longing tugged from within. His mother wished for him school and new parents, a fresh start without the abuse. It was her gift to him from beyond the grave so he could reclaim his childhood. It had been so long since he played with kids his age and learned the basics, such as math, writing and social studies. They would not be a chore for him, for the power had given the insight and intelligence to keep up with and surpass all children in his age category. He could be a college graduate if he wanted, but social skills must be acquired. In order for this to be done he'd need to behave as any ten year old and have a family. The power would guide him to the right people soon enough. There would be no social workers. They'd believe he was their birth son, even if he must assume the identity of another child. A replacement he didn't wish to be, yet forethought already announced the inevitability. To begin he would loiter at the closest elementary school, the one named Godson. He chuckled at the title. He would become God's son with judgment and vengeance at his disposal.

"Come on William, you're gonna be late." Every school morning she was on his case. Monday's were the worst. Of course he went to bed early, but couldn't sleep right away. The two hour bedtime extension on Friday and Saturday nights were more a curse than a blessing and he found himself dragging his feet first thing. Today was Tuesday, yet the grogginess remained. Nightly reading didn't help any, nor did mom's constant worry. She was so paranoid to think he was malnourished or diabetic when the truth was sleeplessness. Sure she checked on him every half hour to make sure he was sleeping, but the fact remained he'd fake it when the floor board outside his room creaked. When she or dad left the room, he'd again prop himself and switch on the battery powered light adhered to his head board. This week's novel was

Stephen King's Fire starter. "Mr. Coleton, get down here." "Yes, mom." he mumbled in reply. He was careful to avoid any aggression in his tone. He slipped into a pair of swim shorts, a tee shirt and socks before scrambling downstairs to the breakfast table. "Did you clean your room?" He rolled his eyes and pictured the toys and laundry scattered on the floor. He'd forgotten to shove them under his bed as usual. "No, mom. After school, kay?" He took his place at the table and stared in discontent at his toast and eggs. No honeycomb, darn it. "I hope you do, because you're not playing outside until it's done." Again he let his eyes roll as he huffed in aggravation. Did other moms badger their kids this way? If he were living at Kenny's he'd be allowed to do as he wished. His mom always gave him room to do as he pleased and even cleaned up after him. Yup, Kenny had the perfect life . . . "And no more of that look, young man. It's disrespectful." He ignored her and nibbled at his breakfast as she packed his lunch. Peanut butter and jam again, with an apple and three cookies. A change would be nice from time to time, but unless the kids at school were willing to trade, he'd be stuck with the same old for another day. Maybe Kenny would bring him taco chips again. He washed down a mouthful of toast with milk and looked to the clock. Twenty minutes until doomsday, the moment he stepped from the car onto the school grounds. As soon as mom drove away, Jaden would be all over him with his usual bullying shoves and ill remarks. He'd probably be wrestled to the ground with his arm twisted behind him until he said 'give' or 'uncle'; one more annoyance to add to his list of morning rituals. One day payback would come and Jaden would get his. Maybe his prayer would be answered and he'd be expelled or transfer schools. Fifteen more minutes and he'd know for sure. When his meal was done he walked his plate to the kitchen sink and washed his hands. Mom collected her purse and keys and they were on their way.

A blue minivan was his target. The boy inside would be the one he'd replace. Donald didn't wish to harm the kid and receded into himself in search of a solution. No, there was only one way. The power knew best. The target would have to be destroyed. With one decision and the power's permission he would be vaporized. He'd feel nothing but an overwhelming peace as he traveled to the heavens to live with God. Mom would see him there. She'd comfort him and be his spiritual mother. It would be a fitting trade off and he'd have nothing to feel guilty for. Regardless of the reassurance, a tear trickled down his cheek as he watched from across the street. Maybe she'd blame him for taking another life, no matter how honorable his intentions. No, she would want this for him. He wiped away the tear and checked for traffic before jogging to the school. The boy jumped from the van and disappeared behind a cedar tree by the front entrance. As his ride drove off, Donald snuck up from behind and studied him. They appeared to be the same age. He was focused on a group of three older kids who were playing a rough game of shove tag. The largest of the group slammed his buddy into the side of the building and shrieked. "You're it!" The kid whispered, "Ouch, that had to hurt," as he parted some branches for a better view. "Whatcha doin'?" At the sound of Donald's voice, the boy gasped and his knees gave way. He landed on his butt and scuttled back against the tree. "Who are **you**?" he asked as he sized up the scantily clothed stranger. Donald held his hand out. "I'm Donald, need help up?" the boy accepted. "Thanks," he said as he stood. He brushed dirt from the back of his shorts and stared inquisitively. "I haven't seen you before. Is this your first day?" "I suppose it is. Were you spying on those guys over there?" He gestured with a glance over to the group. "Oh, that. Yeah, you see the fat one? His name is Jaden. Stay away from him if you value your health. He's a mean prick. I'm William, the class joke. If you want to be unpopular, hang with me for a couple of days. I'll introduce you to Kenny. He's one of the few friends I have in this concentration camp. Where's your shoes? Oh never mind. What grade are you in?" Donald thought briefly before answering. "Five." "Wonderful, you'll be in Mrs. Hemmingway's class. I'll see if I can reserve you a desk by mine." A wry grin crept on Donald's face. "That won't be necessary, yours will be fine." He shut his eyes and imagined the molecules in William's body unraveling. In seconds he'd be vapor. "**My** desk? What do you . . ." His voice trailed off to a soft gurgle. Donald's lids fluttered open. Williams remaining water particles hung like dew on the cedar branches. Using the images in his head, he transformed himself into a perfect replica, including attire. His own mother wouldn't know the difference. Neither would his classmates. Jaden was in for one hell of a rude awakening.

"Glad you could join us William, you're only five minutes late today. You've beaten your own record." Donald stepped from the hall into the classroom. Despite the insecurity rising from his snickering peers, he scanned the room until he found an empty seat. It wasn't difficult to pinpoint once he spotted Jaden. William's desk was directly in front of his, three rows in and second from the front. A timid but good looking blonde girl occupied the seat ahead. Mrs. Hemmingway was just as expected. Curled auburn hair to her shoulders and wire-framed glasses with rectangular lenses, made her out to be more the librarian type. He sauntered past her and took his place. The chair, though hard was comfortable and it felt right to be in it. "One more time mister and I'll be giving your parents a call." He disregarded the comment and she continued. "Take out your spelling books." He reached into the compartment for his books and pens, following his peers' example. As he did he was tapped on the head. It felt like a ruler. He swiveled to face the infamous Jaden. "Yeah," he sneered. "Don't be late again or she'll call mommy on you." So this is how it was going to be. Good to know he saved William from this torment. How long had it gone on, weeks or months? Maybe years, but it would stop permanently before the weekend. "Get lost, jerk." He kept his tone low enough for the teacher to miss. A couple of fellow students heard his comeback and whispered to each other. Though he kept his eyes on Jaden, he knew they were discussing not only his brave new facade, but the consequences he was bound to face for it. Apparently recess was when he'd be 'put in line'. "I'll see you on the playground at ten-thirty," Jaden threatened. "Good." Donald grinned and replied with a witty insult. "I hope you know how to tell time." He turned to face the front of the class and withdrew William's spelling book. The teacher would notice a considerable improvement in the penmanship when she checked his work. To throw off suspicion he'd keep his grade to a 'C' average for a while before gradually raising it. Mom would be so proud. When the lesson had been copied from the board, Donald closed the book and set it aside. Recess was ten minutes away and he chose to read a novel he'd found amongst the mess of papers and snack wrappers in the confined storage compartment. William was in to mysteries, how appropriate. When the bell rang he closed the book and put it away. Jaden was up first and jabbed his shoulder with a fist as he passed. He'd wait for him outside the door and follow him outside. That's when the fun would begin. Before Donald could stand, Mrs. Hemmingway called him over. He stood at her desk and she wrinkled her brow in disappointment. "I don't know what's going on with you lately. It isn't like you to be late for class, yet you have been every day for over two weeks. Your grades have dropped and I'm concerned you may not pass. You don't want to repeat this class next year, do you?" "No ma'am." He reassured with a grin. "I'm sorry for my tardiness. I was having problems, but it's over now. My grades will improve, you'll see. I'll make sure I'm not late tomorrow. Please don't call my mom, I don't want to worry her." Mrs. Hemmingway lay back in her chair and placed her hands behind her head. She took a deep breath and slowly released it. A hint of doubt remained judging by her tired expression, but she overlooked it. "Alright William, I won't call your mother. Don't be late again and bring up your grades by next week or I'll change my mind, got it?" "Yes, ma'am." He assured her. "You won't be disappointed." Confidently he strolled to the door. Jaden was still waiting. Donald ignored him as he passed. Jaden stayed on his heels until he was outside. "Where do you think you're going, coward?" He mocked. When he was clear of the door by several feet Donald turned around. Right to left he glanced to be certain no teachers were watching. A few kids from his class gathered. He didn't wish to cause a scene but still faced his foe audaciously. Jaden shoved his shoulder. He was laughing. "How are you going to avoid being late tomorrow? You gonna hide inside this time?" There was no need to draw the confrontation out any longer. In one swift motion he brought his foot into Jaden's groin and simultaneously latched onto his throat with his fingertips. The grin faded. Jaden fell to his knees holding held his testis, while he groped for Donald with his free hand. His face turned red. More school mates arrived. Some cheered Donald on, others whispered amongst themselves. He hurried things along with a simple warning. "Touch me again and you'll have no need for school, get the picture?" As he struggled to nod Donald shoved him aside and walked away. A few kids followed and praised his bravery while others belittled Jaden. He ignored them all as he headed for the swing set. He could not erase the grin from his face as he recalled the fear instilled in Jaden. It would be a cold day in hell when he bullied another student. As he swung back and forth the power spoke. 'Feels good to have control.' It sure did and he wouldn't lose it again, no matter who paid. Life would be good from now on.

"How was school?" his new mom asked as he climbed in the van. His answer was brief. "Alright I guess." He didn't want to appear overly excited. From recess on, the day had been good. Julie, the girl in front of him passed him a note to compliment his bravery. Jaden kept to himself as expected and Mrs. Hemmingway handed out a surprise test which he aced. She congratulated him on the good work in front of the class which brought a few cheers. Yes, school was good. Mom was proud of him. He felt her spirit encouraging him to continue in his new found confidence. One day he would hold her again and all would be forgiven. For now he'd bask in the attention of his new family. His tummy rumbled. He hadn't eaten for the better part of the day, not since snacking on the hot dogs. William's lunch bag could still be beneath the cedar tree. Why he hadn't thought to seek it out during lunch break was due to excitement. The intoxication brought on by the admiration of his peers. Instead of concentrating on nourishment, he focused on a game of tag. Though he wasn't a very quick runner and lacked some co-ordination, he thoroughly enjoyed the exercise he'd been denied over the years. Yes, things were moving along quite smoothly. "You sound hungry. Didn't you eat your lunch?" "Yes mom," he replied, "I must've burned it off on the playground." "Playground?" Her inquiry emphasized pleasant surprise. "Since when did you decide playing was better than reading?" "Today." He answered. She looked him over. His upright posture was a nice change from his usual self-loathing slouch. "I played tag with my new friend Kenny and a couple other kids." "Don't you mean you're **best** friend Kenny?" Oops, his first slip up. Gotta be more careful or he'd give himself away. He should've researched his prey better. Too late now. No problem as long as he's prudent in the future. "Yeah, that's what I meant. What's for dinner?" The change of subject was the distraction he needed. New mom grinned. "Well, since you've impressed me already once today, I'll let you decide. Just promise me you'll spend more time outside on your breaks. I don't want you growing up a loner." She reached over and tousled his hair. Her touch was soothing and sent warm fuzzies through his body. He could've cried from joy right them. Instead he lay back and let the brilliant sun warm him through the windshield. A content smile graced his lips. He was home. "Okay mom, I promise."

During the next few weeks his popularity at school had grown. One student remained who avoided him at all cost, for now. As promised he was on time every morning much to the delight of Mrs. Hemmingway. Not only had his grades improved, but his social standing caused her to honor him as **most** improved. The title included a gift box with pencils pens and erasers, plus a twenty dollar gift card for Dairy Queen. Everyone was proud of him, everyone but Jaden. From behind his desk he moped as his status dwindled. His grades fell and during lunch and recess he was rarely seen. The roles had been reversed and Donald had received more than he could've hoped for. There was one problem left to resolve. No one else knew of it. Had it not been for the power he'd be unaware himself. From behind him a terrific rage was building and his fate decided. Yes, Jaden was taking jealousy to a whole new level, even to thoughts of murder. Nothing he tried would ease the anger. His small kind jesters provoked the situation further. Was it not selfless to pass Jaden one of his brand new pens? Not in the view of the receiver. The gift was snapped in half and tossed to the floor, which cost Jaden a half hour of detention. And last week when he offered to share his lunch he was rudely told to piss off. Yes there was a violence taking root and any day now it would release itself. One-thirty was P.E. class and as any other rainy day, they headed off to the gymnasium. Today's game was dodge ball and the class was split into two teams. As luck would have it, Jaden was on the opposing side. A menacing smile appeared when he focused on Donald. 'Do nothing' the familiar voice reasoned. He hadn't planned on doing anything but play the game to the best of his ability. Of course Jaden had his own ideas, but surely he wouldn't get **too** out of hand. That's what he believed and that was precisely how the game began. Donald did his best to eliminate every teammate other than the one who attacked no one else **but** him. In his fragile state no unnecessary provocation should be issued, though it would've felt good to pelt Jaden at least once. The game was nearing its finale. Donald's team was down to two, himself and Kenny. Three remained on Jaden's. A ball from Jaden whizzed by his head and slammed Kenny in the shoulder. He was out. The voice spoke again warning him against hostility. He scooped a ball and prepared to throw it at Julie, who was more interested in him than the game. As he focused for a clean shot a hot wave swept through his head. An onslaught of brutal images followed. He weaved on his feet but held his balance. The power had shown him Jaden's mental break. The horrifying visions were of Jaden's plans for him. He couldn't let it happen, he must protect himself. 'Do nothing' the whisper demanded. He knew it was best to obey. If he retaliated now he could lose his good standing. He turned to locate his enemy who had briefly moved from his sights. When he found him it was too late. The ball slammed in hard, snapping his head back and causing instant disorientation. He fell to the floor as the room spun around him. Something wet dripped from his chin. Blood or tears, he wasn't sure. He put is hand to his lip to check and was struck by another round. A whistle blew. The room was fading in and out. He could barely hold himself up. Jaden grabbed him by the collar and swung a right hook . . .

Bright lights shone in his eyes as he attempted to open them. They were heavy and no doubt swollen. He kept them closed and allowed the droning of background noise to lull him to sleep. No point in trying to see through blurry slits anyhow.

"William wake up. Can you hear me?" At first he thought he was dreaming. As he became aware of his surroundings he recognized the woman calling to him. More hazy white light is all he could see. "Mom?" he called. He had made it. He was in heaven and his mother had found him, but why was she calling him William? "It's okay honey, I'm right here." She took his hand in hers. The warm touch was comforting. "Why can't I see, mom? Everything is fuzzy. Can you tell God to help me?" "Oh, William, you'll be fine." 'My name's not William, it's Donald.' He wanted to stress. Flashbacks of earlier that day suddenly jumpstarted his memory and he held back. He was still alive in the real world and his new alias was William Coleton. His real mother would have to wait. "Do you remember what happened?" Of course he did. How could he forget the emptiness in Jaden's stare as his fist smashed his face? "Jaden beat me up." As he spoke a fury began to build. How dare he be ridiculed like this! This wasn't over by a long shot. Jaden would pay, oh yes, he'd pay. "I wanna go home," he insisted. It would've been so easy at that point to transport himself to his new domicile. He only need think it. Unfortunately to do so would expose him and he'd have to begin over again. Besides, the still small echoes of the power continued to remind him to be passive. 'Relax,' it said. 'He'll be taken care of.' Sure karma would likely pay him his due, but that could be years down the road. Something should be done now. "Okay hon. I'll find a doctor to check you out."

An hour later, Donald wobbled through the front door of the Coleton residence. The air smelled of fresh baked muffins and pine cleanser. He made his way to the living room under new mom's guidance and set himself on the chesterfield. "How's your head sweetie?" She cooed as she stroked his dirty blonde hair. "I'll be alright." "Okay then." She rushed off, giving him ample time to explore his surroundings. The layout was no different than any other middle class living room. Across from him

*VISIONS*

a picture window gave him a wide view of the front lawn and driveway. To its right was a large screen television, propped on an ebony wooden stand. The remote lay on the glass coffee table parallel to the couch. He picked it up and pressed the power button. The screen lit up to a soap opera. Not being accustomed to such luxury he watched for a few minutes, and then shut it off. How could anyone delude themselves with such fantasy, he wondered, when all they needed was imagination? New mom returned. In one hand was a glass of milk and the other held a blueberry muffin atop a napkin. She set them down in front of him. "Not watching TV", she observed. "You must've taken quite a hit." He ignored her and picked up the muffin. If only she knew. The past few weeks had been distorted and much of his memory erased. In his efforts to come to terms with how to handle Jaden, he had blanked out the few memories of this house. No, there was more to it than that. Aside from his focus on school he hadn't been home all that often. There were other places to visit; other dimensions in which he wandered to avoid social contact. Those were where his most fond memories lay. School was great, but afterward when he returned home his mood changed. Yes it was nice to have family, but the added attention was confusing. He hadn't needed it at his other house and had grown accustomed to living without it. And now this beating had pushed him further away. There was no need to feel love from others when they would abandon him sooner or later. It was a pattern in all people, so why accept affection at all? Those joyous happy feelings were futile at best. Who needed to feel anyway? Why be disappointed and hurt when it made more sense to accept the situation and deal with it? People for the most part were phony at best; changing their outlook toward each other by the way they made each other feel. Just like Jaden producing his fear in William. He would have kept the poor kid trapped in a life of misery had he himself not taken over. What about Jaden's rage? Look how insignificant it was. All he succeeded at was bringing judgment upon himself. There was anger, sure. A human condition even he could not avoid, but there was also retribution and justice to be carried out. So why would the power dissuade him from doing so? Perhaps it was not all knowing after all. No matter, he'd decide for himself what the jerk deserved, just as he decided his vacation spots. The last one was great. There were no people. No animals, no earth. It was an outer space exploration with him drifting silently around his favorite planets. Why try to explain the complexity of Jupiter and its moons when he could simply study it from as close as he wished? The red spot was not only amazing, but extremely destructive with its hurricane winds and lightning storms. More so, being inside was like being carried away by torrents of rushing water only with rocky debris instead of liquid to propel him along. Good thing he'd imagined himself encapsulated on that trip or he'd have been torn to shreds. So why with all the places he could go, did he stay here? There was really no where else he wished to be for the moment and he'd taken a life to be here. Once that was done he was obligated. So distancing himself was again in the works. Common sense would rule out emotion from now on. Sorry class, no time to socialize. Sorry mom and dad. You'll be lucky if I keep my room clean. He finished his milk and muffin and headed for the front door. Despite his condition, he had work to do. As long as he could still walk and see through the puffiness, he would not slow down until his goal was completed. New

*VISIONS*

mom followed him to the door. For now he'd put up with her pestering concern, but she wouldn't stop him from walking out. "Are you sure you're okay to play outside?" "Yes mom," he muttered. "I'm fine."

Jaden didn't leave school right after the bell rang. He was serving his first hour of detention. Though bored as he was by the lines he was forced to write, he was glad to have his status back. Again the students feared him and he took full advantage. At least three had gone home penniless and hungry after he bled them for their change and lunches. The meddling little twerp who helped earn him the punishment should be out of class for at least a few days. His parents couldn't have cared less about his brawl even though the police had spoken with them. If he hadn't pleaded for another chance he may have ended up in juvenile detention. Amazing how quickly they folded when they realized it. So his sentence had been light, with an extra hour of cursed line writing for the next two weeks. There would be no apology as promised, but he would hold back on running down the goody-two-shoes until he healed. 'I will not fight in school. I will not fight in school . . .' Thirty more to go and he'd read a book. A hundred lines a day was plenty. In twenty more minutes he'd be on his way home. He raised his head. Mrs. Hemmingway was reading a stupid romance novel. She must've finished marking papers and planning tomorrow's agenda. Briefly she glanced up and made eye contact. He lowered his head and continued his work. Man, was she psychic or something? She was tired of him, it was obvious. Though she failed at having him transferred to another class, she would surely make the remainder of the year difficult. So what? If she was too tough on him he'd slash her tires. 'I will not fight in school.' Finally he was done. Satisfied with himself, he reached in his desk for an Archie comic. Ten minutes to go.

School was out forty-five minutes ago. Donald entertained himself by doing what he did best, daydream. On the swing he pictured himself a world-war-two pilot engaged in a dogfight with a Messerschmitt. He rolled his spitfire to line up with the enemy and fired his guns . . . 'go home'. There it was again, the power and its persistent appeal. Why wouldn't it leave him alone? 'Let it go', it urged. No way. Why hadn't it persisted with its passiveness when father abused him, or stayed inert instead of leaping out at mom? What was so damned important about this kid that took prominence over his own flesh and blood? Obviously it couldn't decide between right and wrong and if it did, it sure didn't show it. Maybe the power was simply his own indecisive thinking magnified by his horrendous upbringing. No matter what it was, his mind was made up. In a few minutes Jaden would realize that instilling fear could bring out vengeance in certain people. People who could channel it into unharnessed havoc such as he. If he only knew the scope of what a violated mind could do, he wouldn't step foot from the safety of his house, let alone the school. Jaden wasn't that clever but he'd soon be educated on the flip side of bullying. He should have learned his lesson the first time. Donald slowed the swing to a stop. The power petitioned one last time. 'Think of the consequences'. He had and there'd be none. He was invincible.

"You're free to go, Jaden." "Thank you Mrs. Hemmingway." He placed the three sheets of lines on her desk. "Did you learn anything?" she asked while peering over the rims of her spectacles. "Yes, ma'am." His robotic response was due not to fatigue but by monotony of having to play the remorseful role. He faked a grin and she asked. "And what would that be?" How could he forget? He'd been drilling it in to his head line by line. "No fighting in school." "Good," she said. "Enjoy your afternoon." He sauntered from the class toward the exit. He had just begun whistling as he strolled casually past his old grade three class, and why not? His allowance was due and today was payday. Mom would give him his usual twenty bucks and he'd take a trip on the town this evening. Arcade or movie theater, which should he attend? One was as good as the other and he'd been to the theater last week. Thus his choice was made. He'd go to the arcade for a few games and some ice cream. He arrived at the double door. His hand reached for the release bar but didn't make it. He whirled around to see who had just called him. The hall was empty. He shook his head, not sure if his mind was playing tricks on him. Believing it was, he shrugged and proceeded on his way. His hand fell on the handle and as it did, an icy rush penetrated him to the core. He shuddered and again scanned the corridor. 'Go back'. The urge to turn tail was great. So great he nearly bolted to the furthest exit. No, the fear was all in his head, brought on by mental exhaustion. After taking a deep breath he pushed open the door and cautiously stepped out.

There he was in all his pudgy glory. Donald hauled himself off the swing and headed over. Jaden seemed distracted and hadn't noticed him yet, so he called him over. "Hey Jaden, check out your handiwork," he enticed. "You fat ass garbage disposal." His head shot up. "Looking for your balls are you? Lift up your gut, you slob." Jaden shot him a cold glare. Finally he had his full attention. He took two steps forward, stopped and then surprisingly began to chuckle. Donald was bewildered. What could he possibly be laughing at? Then it occurred to him as Jaden pointed a fat finger at his face. It was the raccoon eyes that got him going. How dare he mock him! He obviously had no idea what he was in for. Donald fought the urge to cry. His emotions were getting in the way. He couldn't let it happen. There was no room for unnecessary distractions and that's all feelings were, a distraction to hinder reason. He forced himself to go numb by focusing on dad, and the satisfaction that came as justice was served. A similar sentence was soon to be unleashed. No different than trapping a mouse that despite you makes your room its own. He'd had that experience two years ago when one came to him in search of food. It was his understanding that they were all disease ridden and there was no way in his weakened state he was taking any chances. He cornered the scrawny rodent and mused over the idea they weren't all that dissimilar. That didn't stop him from flinging it against the wall by its tail. Survival of the fittest he thought when it crunched on impact. Now it was Jaden's turn to be silenced once and for all. "Keep laughing." He said as he stared firmly at Jaden's right arm. His intent was to use the power to bend it behind his back and slam his face to the ground, but as it spoke again to deter him, flashes of the brutal beating erupted along with hatred unknown to most. In that one still second of grief he released the goriest punishment his imagination would allow. Jaden immediately stopped laughing. Something was wrong with his arm. There was pressure as though an invisible hand was clenching his wrist. He attempted to lift it from his side, but it held fast. Despite all effort to think it to action it would not budge. Compression intensified. He couldn't turn away from his bare forearm as bruises formed below the elbow to his hand. They resembled oversized finger prints, like that of a giant. Agony pierced through to the bone and he released a blood chilling scream. He was unaware no one but William could hear him. The boy he tormented had an odd look about him. Something about his face had changed. His flesh appeared to ripple as though struck by high pressured air, yet there was no breeze. His forearm went numb and he returned focus to it as it caved in on itself. The bones began to crush. Flesh tore around the bruising. Blood gushed forth and trickled to his hand. He tried again to pull away, to run form the unnatural presence, but his feet were firmly planted. He was paralyzed, all but his head. Bones ground against each other as the width of his wrist receded. His hand fell off. Vomit spewed from his mouth as his mind fought to accept his predicament. "You see what you get when you play with fire?" Flames danced in William's pupils. He must be possessed by the devil. It was becoming increasingly clear that death would take him and he'd end up in hell like all bad people. No, it couldn't be too late. There had to be a chance for mercy. He had to make the evil in William see that he wouldn't bully again. It needed to understand the lesson was learned. "I . . . I'm sorry. I'll be good." He stammered. The gravel at his feet began to swirl and the ground gave way as if someone had released a drain plug. A vortex opened and widened to his body width. Its edge was mere millimeters from his feet. The glow of hell fire illuminated the hole as thin white smoke plumes streamed skyward. A sinister growl erupted from deep within William's throat. "Too late." The ground under him gave way and Jaden fell. Echoes of terrified screams faded and the ground closed up over him. Donald collapsed to his knees. He was drained but satisfied. Jaden had lived his deepest fear and now it was up to God to decide where he'd spend eternity. He began to snicker at the thought of how relieved his peers would be when Jaden failed to show for class. At least he had no more detention. There's a silver lining after all, but wasn't there always? The best part of the day was the satisfaction of knowing he could override the decisions made by the power. It seemed it would allow him to make his own choice without the threat of consequence. Finally he was in charge. To celebrate, he'd spend some quality time in his favorite dimension; the place with a hot pink sky and purple lawn. He would rest along the bank of the silvery brook and contemplate his next move. He put his hand to his eye. It wasn't swollen. Neither was the other. Jaden's damage had been erased along with him. No one would know the difference. It would be as though he never existed, as it was with William.

"How many times do I have to remind that kid to pick up after himself? It's like he's deliberately disobeying. Are you listening, Henry?" "Yes dear." Mr. Coleton's reply lacked interest. "Good, then set the paper down and let's discuss our son." He did as she asked and folded his hands on the kitchen table. "He's like he's someone else." Sherry sat across from him and sipped her tea. "Come on hon, don't you think that's a bit extreme? He's a kid for cryin' out loud. He's probably testing his boundaries." She set her cup down and sighed. "You could be right but I've been noticing subtle changes in his behavior." Henry rolled his eyes. Sherry sat upright and shook her finger at him. "Yeah, just like that. He doesn't roll his eyes like he used to. I also caught him calling Kenny his **new** friend. They've know each other since first grade." "Yeah, that is a bit strange." Henry had to agree. "But like I said, he's getting older. Soon he'll be going through puberty. Try not to read too much into it." Sherry lay back in the chair and picked up her cup. She took another sip but couldn't relax. There was more to her son's behavior than out of control hormones. Henry wasn't around enough to notice. Perhaps more discipline was needed for him to keep up his chores. Yes, she'd have to put her foot down a little harder next time, starting with his messy room. They would have a nice chat when he came home. Where was he anyway?

Donald awoke from his nap along side the bubbling silver stream. The violet lawn that cradled him had begun to fade to green. The sky as well had returned to its true baby blue tint. Before he could sit up the water receded and in its place several yards away, was the fence which bordered his school. He yawned, stretched and rose to his feet. There was no one around and the sun was headed for the horizon. It must be dinnertime. In ten minutes he'd be walking through the front door and greeting mom and dad with a hug. In twenty-five, all three would be sitting down to a wonderful home-cooked meal. He started across the field to the main road. When he rounded the building he glanced over to the cedar where William had dissolved. Something was shaking the branches. He was compelled to investigate. Softly he drew near. The movement ceased. Whatever it was knew he was there. A bottom limb swayed outward and he stepped back. If it was a wild creature he'd make certain it had plenty of room to pass. All he needed was to be bitten by a rabid animal to end his life in insanity. Not a pleasant way to go. The tree shook again and a small head poked out. It was a young grey tabby. It cautiously stepped forth and ambled over. He sighed with relief and it rubbed itself along his leg. While contemplating whether or not to pet it, he noticed something similar to a fine mist rising from its fur. "You must be one hot kitty," he said as he pulled away. "Go on, get outta here. Find someone else to pester." He turned around and headed home, ignoring the faint cries for affection. It could find someone else to leech on to for all he cared. When he reached the road where it intersected the cross walk, he glanced over his shoulder. The cat had vanished. Thinking nothing of it, he shrugged and continued on.

"It's about time you showed up. Where have you been?" If only she knew. "Sorry mom, I was playing at the park." He wasn't sorry. So what if he was later than she expected? He came back in one piece, didn't he? Next she'd be nagging him to . . .

"I think you should go upstairs and tidy your room. It's long overdue." There it was, just as he pictured. Why should he clean it? **He** wasn't worried about it. Besides, it wasn't too messy. His other room was way worse and he wasn't badgered to keep **it** tidy. If she was so darned concerned she could straighten it herself. Without a word he huffed and headed for the stairs. Sherry watched her son disappear around the corner when he reached the upper landing. Again he hadn't rolled his eyes or even grumbled over the inconvenience. The roast was almost done. He never came home so late, so why the change? Could it be he didn't want to be around her anymore? Had she pushed him that far? Well too bad. If his room wasn't clean after dinner she'd just have to punish him. Grounding from the TV wouldn't wash. He didn't watch it anymore. Strange how a few weeks ago he had given up on it when he used to sit in front of it for hours. Another major variation she had yet to discuss with Henry. The timer on the oven buzzed. By the time dinner was done

*VISIONS*

she had to have a suitable consequence. "How was school today, brat." Henry passed Donald the peas and awaited a reply. "The same as usual and don't call me that. My name is Don . . . William." He accepted the peas while starting at his plate. Sherry and Henry gave each other a discouraging glance. She gave her head a quick jerk toward William as if to say 'see what I mean?' Her eyes narrowed when he nonchalantly rolled his. He knew something was askew, he just didn't care. So maybe the behavior was no big deal at present, but why let it grow into one? Still without his input in the parenting department it would be her will against William's. She didn't need a battle on her hands, she needed family unity. "I'm going for a walk after dinner, okay?" He wouldn't raise his head. "That's alright," she agreed, "provided your room is clean." Donald felt his temper slide. How long was this battle going to go on? It would end now if he had anything to say about it, and he did. "If you don't like the way my room is, don't go in it," he snapped, "or clean it yourself." "William, don't speak to your mother that way." Great, here came the cavalry. "Why not? She's been pestering me every day this week. It's **my** mess and I'll live with it. If you two don't approve, then keep my door closed." He pushed his chair back and stood up. "Next you'll want me doing dishes by hand instead of using the dishwasher." His voice rose with his contempt. "You say you love me, so why don't you prove it? Give me my space . . ." A picture flashed in his mind; a past vision of his former tormentor. He couldn't think straight. He imagined father and the beatings he'd taken. He'd done nothing to deserve them. Suddenly the Coletons didn't seem safe at all. A tear ran down his cheek and before he could stop himself he blurted. "When are the beatings gonna start? How long until you turn into my father?" He ran from the room leaving Henry and Sherry speechless. He could barely see more than a blur as he threw on his shoes. He had to get away and find a safe place, to escape from this horrid reality. Down the street he ran. For the first time since he discovered freedom he'd broken down and as much as he tried, he couldn't cast aside the emotional flood.

"Seriously Henry, we've got to take him to a psychiatrist." For once in his life he didn't cast off her idea. Instead he leaned forward and took her hand. "Looks like dinner's over." "Come on Henry, get serious. Our son needs us. It's like he's having a personality conflict. We have to get him tested. He could be schizophrenic. You heard him. He thinks he has other parents, and abusive ones at that." "Father." Henry corrected. "What?" "He said father, he didn't mention a mom." Sherry yanked her hand away. "Whatever. Somehow he's gotten the idea his 'father' is an abusive monster. Seeing as it couldn't be you 'cause you're rarely home, he's created one. I told you something was up. I'll take him to the clinic tomorrow while you're at work." "Did I sense some resentment because I provide for my family?" He leaned on the table with crossed arms. "Sounds like you're blaming me for his problems." His sternness bore into her. He was right of course, she **was** casting blame. There was no doubt in her mind William was lacking a father figure. It would explain his wavering view of who a father should be and it would be nice if Henry would admit it. Unable to bear the exhaustion of an argument however, she confessed. "You're right, I'm sorry. I'm glad you provide as well as you do, but I think more time is needed with your son. We can't allow him to continue questioning his safety. Still I don't know for the life of me why he thinks we'd hurt him. It has to be mental illness." "That could be." He sighed. "Come on, let's go search for him. I don't want him out after dark."

For over an hour they drove, searching every park and playground. William was no where to be found. Sherry finally spoke, breaking the monotony. "We should call the police." "Not yet." Henry countered. He might still come home. Besides, doesn't he have to be missing twenty-four hours?" "So what do you suggest? We go home and wait?" "Not yet, hon. there's a few more places I'd like to check."

Tears fell to the pool, sending ongoing ripples across the surface. Donald stared at his reflection as it flexed and distorted. He was perched at the end of the diving board, desperately longing for an end to his misery. Over and over he imagined the familiar scenario unfold of his mother falling before floating just below his feet. The continuous 'crack' as her head struck, bounced in his memory like a pinball. There was no freedom for him. The vicious aggressive cycle would continue on for as long as he lived. It's what he'd earned for killing her. Even now it was nearly impossible to imagine any forgiveness from her. He couldn't forgive himself, so why would she? It was proven by his inability to adapt to a trial free existence. There was the bottom line. He hadn't really lived at all, only existed. Going through the motions the way he ought to instead of having it naturally unravel. What was he to do now that he exposed himself? The Coleton's must think he's mentally disturbed. They would send him away to an institution and forget him. There was no unconditional love. People would say they love, but only to get what they wanted. Nothing was free and everyone had an agenda. It was a selfish world and people would use feelings against each other to keep the cycle flowing. The only time a preverbal kink in the wheel would be noticed was when one individual would expect more of another than he or she was willing to put out. Then the table would be lopsided and the system would fall apart. But some were professional and could manipulate well. So well their greed would go either unnoticed or unchallenged. Thus came resentment and the reason for violence. It's what happened when people didn't get their own way. Many a war was fought for such reasons. So what possible balance was there? What was the solution to ending strife? Being alone wasn't it. For some stupid reason people needed each other to avoid being lonely. Maybe it was more like the workings of an ant colony, where every soldier had a purpose to positively affect the others existence. One hand washing the other. Even so, alone time had its benefits, but where to draw the line? Balance was needed; a balance of emotion and common sense. Knowing when to help and when to back off was crucial. There was none amongst the chaos of his life. His world had a permanent wobble, with every decision wrought with confusion. Where to go now? Attempt another go with the Coletons? A world of his own creation looked brighter, but it was nothing more than illusion. The real world was disillusion. Go forward, go back? Around people or away from? What started as a dream come true had twisted to a nightmare. Until he knew for sure which choice was best he would stay put. "Help me." He whimpered, hoping either mom or the power would show him the way. There was one final option. Join mom in the heavens and live an eternity in bliss with her. 'Heaven is within.' A gentle voice replied. It was neither the power nor mom. Though similar to mom's it had a more internal impression. Perhaps it was his own spirit, though he doubted it was. He didn't have the ability to reason such a thought, so it must be God.

Whether God, mom, the power or himself, he knew what he must do. He would meditate and search internally for the best direction. Until then he would stay where he was, the closest place possible to mother.

"Don't worry honey, he'll show up." Henry wrapped his arm over his wife's shoulder as they made their way up the walk. She shivered from the cool night air. "I can't help it. I want my baby home." They reached the door and he fished out his keys. "Should we call the police now?" She asked with noticeable worry in her tone. Her facial expression reflected the same. He led her over the threshold, uncertain of what to say. It wasn't that he didn't want to alert the authorities of his son's disappearance. He knew if he did they'd tell him what he already expected, wait until morning. "You know what they'll say. I'll make you a cup of herbal tea to help you sleep." He stepped into the kitchen ahead of her and switched on the light. "Oh great," he exclaimed while grimacing from the sight of dinner dishes. "Have a seat." He told her. "I'll get to those in a minute." "Nonsense, I'll clean up. I have to occupy my mind somehow." Henry filled the tea kettle and set it on the stove. He turned up the heat then turned to his wife. She was busy wrapping leftovers. Each dish she cleared he loaded into the dishwasher. She placed the remaining food in the fridge and rinsed out a dishcloth to wipe off the table. When it was clean she tossed the rag in the sink and sat down. When the kettle whistled, Henry set it on a cold burner and dropped a chamomile bag into a cup. He poured the water, set the cup on a saucer with a spoon and set it before her. She thanked him and he sat across from her. The next hour or so would be spent engaged in idle chit chat. Neither of them would have much sleep tonight.

Sherry awoke on the couch. The bleep of the phone had awakened her. The television was on without volume. Henry must have muted it before he went either to work or bed. She grabbed the remote and checked the time. It was ten-thirty. Wearily she slid along the couch to the end table and lifted the receiver. "Hello?" She asked, hoping William was on the other end. "Hi, is this Mrs. Coleton?" "Mmm, yes it is. Who's this?" She lay against the armrest and stretched her legs over the coffee table, yawned and waited for the woman to continue. "Hello, Mrs. Coleton, I'm your son William's teacher. He isn't in class today. Will he be attending this afternoon?" Sherry sat up and grabbed the receiver with both hands. "No, I mean I don't know. He didn't come home last night." There was a pause and then, "Mrs. Coleton, are you aware that William's grades have drastically improved in the past couple of weeks? He's gone from a low 'C' to 'B' plus average. In my four years of teaching I haven't seen anything like it. Is he doing anything at home that could account for it, extra homework perhaps?" "No, not that I've noticed . . ." She thought for a moment before continuing. "He has been acting differently though. We got into an argument last night and he ran away. It's like his personality has completely changed, like he's not really my son." "Have you considered taking him for an evaluation? I have the number of a good psychologist. He specializes in children and comes highly recommended." Sherry considered her options while Mrs. Hemmingway waited quietly. William **should** see a specialist, but would he come home? He could be hurt somewhere; scared and lonely . . . Then again he may soon show up here or at school. "Okay, hold on while I grab a pen and paper." Less than a minute later she was back on the line. Mrs. Hemmingway read out the doctor's name and number. After writing it down, she said, "Call me if he returns to class. I'll come and pick him up." "Immediately," she replied. Sherry thanked her and hung up. She stared at the number, debating if calling right away would be too spontaneous. She chose to wait for her son. Doctor Kueber would have to wait. On her way to the washroom to freshen up for the day, she mulled over her phone conversation. Though disappointed in William's actions, she was quite proud of his academic success. If he could overcome his emotional issues, she'd have the perfect son.

Donald paced along the edge of the lake. After returning to the new town he fought with the decision to return to school or home. His depression had waned by sunrise and he was willing to try again to make a go with Sherry and Henry. He would clean his room as soon as he could and end all arguments. Everything would be put right. As far as his outburst, he would explain it away as a nightmare he had the previous night. He may have to endure counseling sessions, but they wouldn't persist for long. His fresh attitude would see to that. He would become the best student and son he could be, now that he was free of any distractions. So where to go from here? School was preferable, though under the circumstances, home would be wiser. Mom and dad were undoubtedly flustered by his vanishing act. By now they were likely searching high and low. They may have called the authorities. Yes, home would be better. No point in drawing any further attention his way. Two ducks, a male and female flew toward him from across the still water. As they neared they descended to head level and aimed for the patch of lawn behind him. He studied them as they cleared the lake. They were waist high when they soared by, missing him by less than six feet. He laughed when they touched down and seemingly tripped over their own feet. "Not very stylish." he said aloud when they nearly ended up on their beaks. What clumsy birds they were, and not too bright. They squabbled amongst themselves and headed for him. He knew they wanted food. Wow, he hadn't thought about eating until now. "Sorry, I'm as hungry as you are." They didn't care and came up to him anyway. He held out an empty hand. The male moved in and snapped at his finger. Again he chuckled and straightened up. "Stupid birds." He said. "If I had a fire you'd be dinner, now beat it. I have my own food to find." He headed for home, with the ducks following. They began their chatter and he took offence. "Can't you take a hint?" Ungrateful animals! They must be gossiping about him to each other. That is how they behaved, as though he owed them something. Well he'd give 'em something alright. "I said beat it!" He yelled as he spun around. His shoe came up and nearly clipped the beak of the female. She squawked and turned tail, wings clumsily flapping for balance. That was when he noticed it, a thin mist rising from both of them. He thought of the kitten. This city must have an unusual humidity problem. Bewildered by the phenomenon, he shook his head and walked toward the parking lot. As with the cat, he looked back after several paces. The birds were nowhere to be seen. The likelihood of them flying or waddling for cover was improbable. They had no time to clear the area and they hadn't flown. He would've heard the beating of wings. Strange how no other creatures were present. No other ducks, no geese. Not even a crow, as though some hidden danger was present that he'd suddenly become unaware of. 'You're reading into it too deep.' He told himself. 'Be rational.' A chill coursed through him beginning in his chest then spreading to his limbs and head. He shuddered and picked up the pace.

Sherry Coleton set the three plates she had taken from the dishwasher into the cupboard as the doorbell rang. She wiped her damp hands on the dishtowel, set it on the counter and rushed to answer it. Hopefully it would be good news. Secretly she thought the worst. The police were about to inform her of William's injury or death. Silently she mouthed a quick prayer and slowly turned the knob. "Is that you, mom?" The familiar voice caused her heart to pound with excitement and she swung the door open. There was her son, dirty, haggard but alive. Bending to her knees she took him in her arms and pulled him close. Too close. "Mom, I can't breathe." She released him and held him at arms length. "Where were you? Your dad and I were worried sick." She didn't wait for a reply. "Come to the kitchen. I'll make you something to eat after I call you dad. He'll be so relieved." When she lifted the receiver he sighed. It was nice to be home again, even though he couldn't help but ponder future consequences. Suppose 'dad' wasn't relieved as much as disappointed? He could make it a tough go with extra grounding and chores. Time would tell. "Yes dear, he's fine," she relayed to her husband as she took a seat. "I'm about to make him lunch . . . yes, yes, later. I'd rather wait so we could tell him together." Her hand hid her mouth. She must've thought he was deaf or something. Yeah, it sure looked as if dad had already planned punishment. "I love you too. See you around six." She hung up and faced him, was about to say something, but changed her mind. Instead she stood and went to the fridge. She was hiding something. "How about a roast beef sandwich?" He disregarded her and cocked an ear for that tremor in her speech that gave away tension. "Or salmon?" There it was, hardly noticeable, but it was there. Anyone else would've missed it; then again they wouldn't be listening for it. Her back was to him and he glared with contempt. How dare she plan something concerning him and hide it! Whatever it was better not be harmful or so help her . . . She emerged from the fridge with sandwich fixings and laid them on the counter. "I bet you're starving hmm? Well, not for much longer." She wouldn't look at him. What was with her condescending tone? It was starting all over again. Couldn't she talk to him like an adult, or at least without lording over him? How could he look up to her when she wouldn't treat him like an equal? 'Don't patronize me bitch.' He wanted to say. His palms began to sweat and his breathing grew heavy. The things he could do to her . . . His jaw tensed and he ground his teeth. 'Don't you dare.' She turned around and he swiveled in his chair. He wouldn't make eye contact for fear the power would strike her down. Instead he took a deep breath and forced himself to relax. "Here you go sweetie, roast beef with lettuce, tomato and mayo, just as you like." No, that's what William liked. Any food was preferable to him, Donald Louis Faven. The charade was wearing on him. It sucked not being able to be himself. Every time his own characteristics shone through his sanity was put into question. Still he had to play the game. Perhaps one day he'd become accustomed to his role, but for now he'd keep quiet and eat his sandwich. His stomach growled as he took the first bite. Mmm, delicious. Maybe when he was full he wouldn't feel so grumpy. Afterward he'd take a nap and when he awoke, he'd clean his damn room for no other reason than to impress his care takers. 'Mom' watched him until he was half way through, and then went to the dishwasher to empty it. "Please put your plate in the machine when you're done." When she was finished she brought him a glass of milk. "Thanks mom." She smiled and headed for the living room to watch TV. Yeah, he had some control after all. Dad would be tougher to break but he'd succeed. A little planning and a few weeks ought to do it, no problem.

The sun was already setting when he awoke in his room. Donald yawned and stretched before climbing out of bed. He still wore the tee shirt and jogging pants he'd had on for the past two days. If he didn't come off as ratty before, he sure did now. 'Dad' would likely comment on his scruffy apparel and unkempt hair. He didn't know the man well but he portrayed himself as the uppity, proud type. His slick dark hair was parted to the right like an English businessman. A prim and proper chap he was, minus the 'pip pip, cheerio' banter and accent. A typical arrogant prick that had to pretend to be somebody, so his low class sales position didn't look so pathetic. He could hear them down the hall, chatting over petty things like bills and insurance payments. Stepping from his room he followed their voices to the living room. "Well, well, look who's up. Have a good sleep son?" Damn it Henry, enough with the cynicism already. "Yeah, how was work?" "Oh you know, same as usual. Have a seat would you?" Donald shifted his attention from dad to mom. "Family meeting?" He curtly asked before plopping on the couch beside her. Dad leaned forward in his recliner. "Yes as a matter of fact. I'll be blunt. Your mother and I would like an explanation as to your behavior yesterday. It's not like you to speak out at us like you did, so tell us what's been bothering you." He squirmed in his seat. What could he say, other than the lie he'd dreamed up earlier? He'd stick with it for lack of a better story. "I've been having nightmares. I guess because they were so vivid I believed them. I should've told you before. I'm sorry." A sorrowful pout should put them at ease. The parents glanced to each other and he marveled at the confusion in their expressions. "Are you sure that's all?" Sherry asked. She wasn't quite convinced and neither was Henry. He nodded vigorously. "Just to be on the safe side, how would you feel if we have a doctor check you out?" The suggestion came from Henry. No surprise there. 'How would you feel if I rip your puny brain from your head and hand it to you?' he wanted to say. It was after all, the same idea as being mentally probed by a so-called specialist. Instead he sheepishly smiled and replied, "Okay." It was enough to make Sherry sigh with relief. "Good, then you'll take the day off school tomorrow. Mom has already set up the appointment." Wow, that was quick. Nice of him to ask **after** the fact. They didn't have to sugar coat it. It was more insulting than telling him the engagement was set and he was going regardless. When would adults ever learn? "Now clean your room before dinner." Geez Henry, could you possibly rub more salt in the wounds? He bit his lip and headed off. As he left he heard Henry say, "I don't know about that kid. He sure keeps me guessing." "Get used to it dad," he said under his breath, "There's a lot more to come."

The next morning came quick. Heavy winds blew rain against the bedroom window. He leaned his head on the glass and peered outside. The down spout at the corner of the roof had dislodged and a steady stream poured from it. A perfect start to a bullshit day. Mom was scurrying about the kitchen. Clanging dishes gave away the fact she was cooking breakfast. Dad had left for work some time ago, so she must be sucking up, like giving a dog a treat before a trip to the vet. What was the point of this flood of concern? It's not as if he took up smoking or drug use. Hey, now there's a topic that would make some interesting conversation. Definitely it would give the shrink something to mull over. It would also set mom off. Ah, heck, no need to torture the ol' girl. Besides the last thing he needed was to be dragged to rehab or checked into a nut ward. He'd stick to his nightmare story. The smell of frying bacon jogged him from his daydream. He pushed himself away from the depressing sight and headed for the kitchen. He was wearing his pajamas still. His test for mom. Would she send him back up to change or let it go? If he was sent up, she was self confident. If not her meekness would show through. If that was the case, she'd go along with almost anything he did or said to prevent causing waves. Yes, it was a crappy day but it still had its moments. He entered the kitchen. "Morning mom", he said cheerfully. As yesterday, she evaded eye contact. Something about him made her nervous. "Good morning. You're in for a treat. Bacon and eggs with toast and juice. I'm sure you'd prefer honeycomb, so I'm giving you a choice." "Bacon and eggs is fine." Wow, she must be frightened. Could it be she knew more than she let on? Most likely, but to what extent? Was it possible she saw through his guise? He should've taken the cereal. Too late now. "So when is my appointment?" Sherry placed his breakfast before him. Finally she looked at him. It was obvious she was exhausted. She probably hadn't slept a wink. The skin under her eyes sagged and red veins snaked over the whites. "Just over an hour, now eat up. I have to get ready." She said no more and left the room.

Raindrops leapt off the pavement as they pounded down. During the drive he allowed the pelting on the windshield to lull him to a catatonic state. Neither he nor she spoke for the duration of the trip. There wasn't much to say anyhow. All the talking would be done in the doctor's office.

His shoes were beginning to leak at the sides and he did his best to avoid puddles as he hastened ahead. Once under the shelter of the entrance he waited, but only a second. Sherry was right on his heels. She reached around him and grabbed the metal handle of the glass door. "You first," she insisted. She struggled to smile. Why bother? They both knew something was up. Unlike him she had no proof, and that's why they were here. Once in the waiting room, Donald headed for the table with reading material and 'mom' talked to the receptionist. "You can come right in," she said as he reached for a Popular Mechanics magazine. His hand fell to his side and he followed the two women down a narrow corridor to a small office. "Have a seat. Doctor Kueber will be with you shortly." There were two vinyl covered chairs on the far side underneath the window and he sat in the closest one. Sherry squeezed between him and the doctor's desk. He moved his legs to accommodate her. She didn't sit right away, but chose instead to stare out into the parking lot. "It'll be okay mom, I'm not crazy or anything." Her lips moved as though answering him but no words were formed. He studied each movement and determined what she meant to say. "That remains to be seen." So much for faith in her child. That did it. No more 'I love you.' No more trying to fit in and no more hoping for acceptance. There wasn't going to be any on either of their parts. If she couldn't believe in him, then he'd have no trust in her. Kueber entered the office. Sherry turned from her dismal distraction and introduced herself. When they had shaken hands she motioned to him. "This is my son,

William." "Yes, I hear you're having some difficulty lately young man. Would you like to tell me about it?" Well here was his chance to put Sherry in her place. He'd have to be subtle. "I've had nightmares, that's all." The doctor rubbed his chin and leaned his elbows on the desk. "Could you describe them?" He thought back to the disagreement that caused this problem. He shouldn't have spewed off about his fears. Now he had to relive them. "It was nothing really. There was a man who hurt me. It was just a dream. It's no big deal." "No big deal?" Sherry suddenly spat. "How could you call it no big deal? You ran away for cryin' out loud." The doctor raised his hands. "Okay Mrs. Coleton, please relax. Let's hear him out first and then you can have a turn." She sat back and crossed her arms like a spoiled child. It was time to turn the tables and take the focus off himself. "You know," he began, "now that I think of it, things haven't been too good at home. Dad's never around and I don't have many friends. I spend a lot of time alone. It would be nice to do more as a family." Sherry's eyes opened wide and her jaw dropped. The urge to speak must've gnawed at her something fierce. Too bad, she could have the floor soon enough. "How do you feel about your father?" Kueber picked up a pad and pen. Donald put on his best sad face. "He's too serious. The only time we talk is when he's telling me what he wants from me. We never have regular conversations. I feel like I always have to please him. That puts a lot of stress on a kid my age, know what I mean?" "I understand. Keep going." Kueber's pen never left the paper. "It would be nice to play ball and stuff like that. Instead all I hear is 'clean your room' and 'have you done your chores?' Why can't he take an afternoon for me?" "May be if you did your chores once in a while you'd . . ." Kueber raised a finger to his lips and Sherry fell silent. His hand feverishly scribbled notes. She frowned and tried for a closer peek but one look from the doctor and she huffed and turned away. "So you feel rejected, is that safe to say?" Donald nodded. "Okay, now that we have your side we'll hear from your mother. Go ahead Mrs. Coleton." She smiled and gave Donald the evil eye. "I can't believe you'd blame your father for your behavior. Mr. Kueber, you don't know us well but, if you did you'd know my husband's a loving man. How William ever got into his head that he's some kind of abusive monster, I'll never know. Plus it doesn't explain other changes like the sudden lack of interest in television, nor his grade improvements. Doctor, if I didn't know any better, I'd swear he's not my son." Finally, a taste of honesty. "That was mean, mom." Donald pouted. Inside he was laughing. Now he knew that she knew but couldn't confirm it. "Yes, well at least I said it. Doctor, I want drug tests. Something's changed my son and I'd like to know what." Wow, it was like she could read his mind. At this rate he wouldn't have to say much more. She'd said enough for them both. Kueber dropped the pen and folded his hands. "First of all Mrs. Coleton, I think you should listen to yourself. Don't you think your distrusting thinking might play a part? Children are sensitive to parental reaction and any hint of rejection can change their behavior dramatically. I'm going to recommend counseling for the both of you. I suggest you take your husband along whenever possible. I'll make a note for your family doctor and prescribe drug tests for both of you. I'll have him fax me the results. And Mrs. Coleton, try to get along in the meantime. Remember, you're the parent so set a good example. That's all for now." He stood and held out his hand. Donald shook it and thanked him. Sherry stared dumbfounded. Obviously the discussion wasn't what she'd expected. Reluctantly she shook Kueber's hand and ushered Donald through the corridor.

"How dare you!" She slammed the door so hard Donald jumped in his seat. "You made us out to look like criminals. Wait 'til your father finds out. I hope he gives you the belt." It would never happen. Not only would he prevent it, he'd severely punish anyone who tried. Of course he made them appear abusive. The way she carried on would be disruptive to **any** child. Not him though. He knew how to play the game, and what she got was what she had coming. Whose fault was it they ended up at a shrink's office? Any normal parent would say, 'okay son, let's talk,' not 'you're broken, I'm taking you to the repair shop.' Drug tests, now there's a laugh. Hope you haven't been pounding back the cough syrup again, mummy dearest. He snickered as she turned the key. "What's so bloody funny? You planned this whole thing didn't you?" He wanted to say 'yeah, with your help,' but thought better of it. Instead he smirked and reclined the seat. Sherry's phony behavior was showing through. She was no sweeter than the next person. As with everyone, she didn't have the perfect little life she tried to display. What she did have, were past regrets she hadn't dealt with. Too bad her baby boy was flawed. It would give her something to work for instead of having everything handed to her on a silver tray. If she wouldn't take the steps to be an understanding mother, she ought not to expect success. That's how life was. "I know you did something with my William. Who are you?" And there it was, the truth exposed. "But mommy, what on earth do you mean?" He smugly replied. "Don't play games with me," she shot back. "Don't you think I know my own son?" He studied her for a moment. Suppose he let her in on his little secret? Who'd believe her? She'd be labeled a loony at the drop of a hat. She couldn't prove any of it and maybe if she knew, she'd come to accept him. The way things were now it wasn't going to happen. "Okay," he said. "Suppose for a moment that I'm **not** your son." Sherry pulled to the curb. The rain had eased to a light drizzle. She shut the wipers off and shifted to park. Her attention was on him, so he obliged her by raising the back rest. He unbuckled his safety belt and angled himself to face her. She wasn't frightened or angry. At best she was relieved. "Okay then, who might you be if you're not my William?" "Well I don't know," he toyed. "I might be an angel sent to knock you off your high horse. So how old were you when your mom and dad separated?" He'd caught her off guard. He was only guessing but he must've got it right. "How'd you . . . alright, stop analyzing me. I can tell you're quite clever, but I'm sure you're no angel. Enough with the games." She pursed her lips and glared. "Okay Sherry, hope you can handle the truth. Here goes. I'm nobody. A kid William's age who never had a chance. No school, no friends. My dad used to beat me you know. Other things too. He was quite the bastard." There it was, all laid out in the open. No more hiding or messing with her feelings. Sadness filled the void left by his arrogance and a tear came to his eye. The rest of his story spilled out unhindered, exposing him and leaving him at her mercy. He didn't want to let it out, it just happened. "You wanna know me so bad, why don't I tell you about my mother. I loved her but she died. It's my fault, but she's in heaven now. She sent me to you, to William. I'm sorry about your son Mrs. Coleton, but he wasn't happy anyway. I bet you didn't know he was being bullied every day at school. Why do you think he was late for class all the time?" Sherry gasped and put her hands to her mouth. "Are . . . are you telling me my son is dead?" Donald simply grinned. "And you're a spirit that took over his body? Oh my god, I can't believe what I'm hearing." "Not a ghost Mrs. Coleton. I didn't die, William went away. I simply took over his body. Well, not **his** body. I copied it for my own. You wouldn't have taken me in as Donald, so I became William. Sorry I did such a lousy job copying his mannerisms. I can't help who I am." Sherry shook her head unwilling to accept his account, but just as he couldn't deny himself, neither could she. She only needed time for it to register. "Donald, is that your name? It makes sense now . . ." She must be thinking back to his slip up. "Do you have a picture? What do you look like?" They were communicating. Not as mother and child, but as one human to another. This is what was needed to build the bonds of friendship. Putting all fears aside he chose to do something he swore he wouldn't. It needed to be done to seal their commitment. "Close your eyes, Sherry." Her hands fell to her lap. "What for?" She was still a little leery. "Trust me. You want to see me as Donald, well I'll show you. Now close them. I'll tell you when to open them." Reluctantly she did as he asked. "No peeking now." She shook her head. Donald covered his face with his hands and pictured his true portrait, as he'd seen it in the reflection of the lake. That was the first day he'd arrived in the city and the first time in years he saw his true appearance. How could he forget that broken, ragged child? Slowly he pulled his hands away. He could feel the change by the way his skin crawled and stretched. He plucked a hair from his head. It was dark brown, not dirty blonde. Quickly he yanked the rear view mirror his way. There he was in his true form. The boy with a broken soul caked in scars. The view was painful, too agonizing to look at. He pushed the mirror away and took a deep breath. "Okay Mrs. Coleton, you can open them." Sherry squinted as though staring into sunlight. Her lids rose deliberately slow in anticipation of Donald's real traits. He must not have been what she expected. When her eyes were fully open she just looked on curiously. No words were spoken immediately. Instead she reached out and touched his face. "But how?" She asked while caressing his cheek. "This is impossible." "No Mrs. Coleton," he corrected. "This is reality." She looked on I awe for a moment more, and then as though over whelmed by it all, she broke. Instead of inquisitive, she became angry and slapped his cheek. "You murderer, you killed my son!" She turned for the door handle but he grabbed her wrist. He wasn't angry as he should've been. Numbness removed his emotion for good reason. To be irrational now would mean her destruction and having to start over. There was too much invested to throw it all away. She reached out to scratch his arm but upon sight of his void, shiftless gaze she changed her mind. Perhaps she realized the futility of her position. If her son could be so easily replaced, then maybe she could too. "Where's his body? I want to see it. I need to." Her pleading would do no good. "You can't, he's gone." "Gone where?" She nervously glanced around, avoiding eye contact. "I don't know. I wished him away and he vaporized. I can't help you, but I can be your son all the same." With one thought he was William again. The transformation had a soothing effect. Sherry went limp and rested her head on the steering wheel. "Alright." She sighed. "Let's get home." She started the van and pulled away from the curb. The rain had stopped. He was glad she'd given in. They would live well together and he'd be a good son.

*Can he read my thoughts? Oh my lord, what if he could? Okay, instead of getting all worked up, test a theory. Think 'I hate you'. Twenty seconds, twenty five . . . No response. Alright, he doesn't seem to have that ability. Oh jeez, he's smiling like nothing's changed. How could he just forget about it? He must be a sociopath. He'd have to be to admit so freely to killing his own mother. What would it take to set him off again? Let's hope it's nothing I say or do. No telling how far his disturbing intellect would take him. The consequences could be catastrophic. Still there has to be some way to get rid of him. Show no fear, no meekness. Remember, for now he's William. To everyone, he's the son I bore ten years ago. Nothing's changed, nothing . . . Not too easy to convince yourself, is it Sherry? Oh man, it's gonna be tough not to picture his real face every time he acts up. How can he be disciplined without a negative reaction? Take it slow, Sherry. Take it slow . . . Have to watch him carefully. The punishments would have to be light. He had to believe he was loved as our own. Perhaps in time he'd settle in as part of the family . . . No! He was no better than a common intruder. Remember, William is dead. He's gone for good. Don't think about it too much or it'll bring nothing but heart ache. Henry should know. Oh lord, how do I tell him? Was it best to keep him in the dark? For now, yes. Until I figure out what to do with this imposter, it is best to remain silent. Keep it a secret, mine and Donald's, uh, William's. Gotta watch it, can't use the wrong name. Henry would know for sure something was amiss. He's awfully quiet. What must he be thinking? By his expression the deception is working. Good, let him think he's safe. For now he will be, but he'll slip up eventually. What about his weaknesses? So* *far he hasn't shown any other than the breakdown he had before running away. That's it; he'd have to be in that head space again before he would leave. Henry would have to bare witness in case he **wouldn't** leave. That was the key, the answer needed. Somehow he would have to fall into a depression deep enough for everyone to notice. Then he could be disposed of with little attention drawn. Maybe poisoned or struck over the head. Once dead it would take no more than an hour drive to dump the body. Far enough away that it'll take some time to be discovered. Then claim he ran away again. It was perfect! Almost home. We should go for lunch and get to know each other better. Well enough to tell when it would be wise to mention his real father. Yeah, that would catch him off guard. Hopefully then he'd sink away into his past life and find that emptiness he wanted to run from. So that was it. Finally, a perfect plan to help him leave on his own. Go after him if he chooses to run. After all, he murdered my William. Chase him down and run him over until his skull shatters from the weight of the car. It's almost too perfect . . .* "Say, why don't I take you someplace nice for lunch? Your choice. Maybe we could start again and get to know each other." *Wow, what a big grin. He had all his adult teeth, just like William.* "Sounds good . . . mom."

Nothing like a teen burger after a life altering experience. Donald sipped his root beer before nibbling at his fries. Sherry sat beside him, studying his every move. There was no reason for her to take such interest, as she couldn't have cared less an hour ago. Was she really concerned or preventing problems? Perhaps she needed to figure him out to decide the best way to answer Henry's questions. He was bound to ask not only about the quality of his day, but of his health as well. She'd no doubt answer subtly to ease his curious mind. The better he figured the family to be, the less he'd pry into their lives. He wasn't really much of a father anyway. More like a dictator or captain running a ship; a part-time commander and nothing more. At least he was beginning to appear that way. Perhaps he was prejudging and his views were based on opinions he held for the dad he'd grown up with. It didn't really matter which direction his beliefs wandered. All men were the same. God forbid he end up that way. It would be preferable to die . . . There was no point in going home immediately. He needed time for himself away from Sherry. Something about her new found acceptance was off, as though she hadn't really made up her mind. Still, the die was cast and she'd have to come to peace with the situation as it was. "I'd like to go to school. There's still half a day." She nodded and remained expressionless with the exception of a Mona Lisa smile. From the restaurant she neither spoke nor glanced his way, until they arrived at the front parking lot of the school. She had much on her mind to contemplate. So did he. "Tell Mrs. Hemmingway thank you for her patience." He opened the passenger door. "And be good. Would you like a ride home?" "No thanks, I'll walk." He stepped out and closed the door. Sherry waved with her fingers like a school girl with a crush. He waved his hand in a semi solute and dropped it to his side. "Whatever." He mumbled before heading in.

"How nice to see you, William, I wasn't expecting you in today." "Mom says hi," he said as he passed her desk. There was no need for pleasantries. He reviewed the subjects for the day. Spelling and P.E. were over, leaving math and whatever test the teacher had in mind. He glanced around the room. The students hardly took notice. They were working on an art project of sorts.

"It's free art day, William. Use your pencil crayons and create a picture of whatever comes to mind. Make it as imaginative as possible." Hemmingway brought over a few sheets of blank paper. "You can use these to make a few small pictures or combine them into one large one. Have fun." Fun, yeah creativity was fun alright. Let's see, how about drawing up some recent events such as Jaden's battle by the swings. Yeah, and what else? Something to do with the future, and a family portrait from the past. That should earn him a 'B+' for sure, maybe an 'A'. For an hour he drew up his masterpieces, his hands flailing as though possessed by an angry soul. He thought of violinists grinding the bow over the strings in a fury. Dark octaves would fly into the air in a massive spray, before raining down into the ears and hearts of the audience. They, like he could understand the intensity, the vigor spilling forth from a tormented spirit. It was beautiful. "Okay class, you have ten minutes until the bell. Please drop your drawings on the corner of my desk before you leave." Ten minutes? Wow, time flies when enthralled in work. There was hardly enough time left, but as the bell rang his final stroke was laid and the pencil crayon dropped to the table. He leaned back and placed his hands over his head. When he gazed down he couldn't believe his hand had done the work. Before him in an abstract design, were memories of the past and one vision of the future. The first drawing showed his birth father with a beer in hand and behind him, a corridor with a door at the end. His face, Donald's face poked from the partial opening. There were tears on his cheeks. The next showed Jaden staring into the well of hell in which he'd fallen into. Beyond was an empty swing set. Very impressive and realistic they were with their three dimensional semblance. The third was curious to say the

*VISIONS*

least. There he was in . . . Strange; he hadn't noticed the blob in the corner. Slowly he leaned forward to study the sketch closer. There was a shadow to the upper right of the page. No features, just two empty spaces that resembled eyes. And what of him? He appeared to be in pain. How could this be? Didn't he start with new mom on her knees and he with a whip in hand? He intended it to be a joke, but it didn't come out the way he was sure he'd drawn it. And what of the room he was in? Large tubes resembling inverted beakers with ghostly images swarming around. It wasn't what he'd drawn at all! It was . . . "Time to go William, bring me your papers." When he looked up he discovered he'd been lost in thought. The classroom was vacant with the exception of the teacher. The chorus of students which resounded from the hallway, began to fade as they made their way homeward. Donald organized the sheets in order, with the picture of the shack and his former dad on top. Suddenly he wished he hadn't done the art project. There was something unnerving and all too real about all of them. Despite them being impressive enough for any art gallery, they had an air of reality to them. Not the reality he'd planned, but one created for him by an unknown source. No, it couldn't be. It was probably just a slip, a daydream put to paper. He walked them over to Mrs. Hemmingway and set them on the pile. "See you tomorrow Mrs. Hemmingway." "William, can I have a word?" He stopped and faced her. "You look sad, is something troubling you?" Of course there was. Look at the art project. It says it all. "No ma'am, I'm just tired, I didn't sleep well. I'm sorry I was late." She smiled but her worry showed on her brow. "That's okay. I know you've had trouble at home. I had a chat with your mom." He hung his head. "We're fine now." He muttered. "Thanks for your concern. I should get going." He started for the door, dragging his feet as he went. He was drained alright, but not from lack of sleep. Something about the drawings was taking his energy. "William?" He turned his head. Hemmingway wore a sorrowful frown as though disturbed by his reaction. She was genuinely distressed by his discontentment. Could it be she had true compassion for him? Her mother instinct must be working overtime. "If you ever need to talk, I'll listen." 'Sorry' he wanted to say, 'my problems are out of your league.' Instead he said a simple thank you and left the room. When he was gone, Mrs. Hemmingway thumbed through the drawings beginning with his. "Impressive," she said aloud as she lay them side by side in front of her. She examined them closely, noting the detail. These pictures were good, really good. How unfortunate to see how depressing they were. Not one portrayed anything positive. William wasn't out of his funk yet. Give it time; there was a long way to go. It was simply a phase he was going through. All children went through it, especially gifted ones. Perhaps he needed more of a challenge. She'd work with him to meet his needs. It was wonderful to see him blossom so rapidly. Rare, but wonderful.

Where was the power? He hadn't sensed it since Jaden's fiery demise, so where had it gone? More importantly, would it be there when required? Again he had stopped by the lake on the way home, only this time he headed to higher ground. In the wooded part of Centennial Park he rested while deciding on a destination. The purple place was wearing out its welcome and there was no will to attempt another outer space adventure. The Jupiter trip was way over the top. Dizziness still plagued him when he thought about it. It was difficult to fathom he'd been there for real. Where he **had** gone was his own version of the planet, a vision created through the knowledge he'd obtained through books and beliefs. Where to go now? Well, he'd just have to allow his imagination to soar to wherever it pleased. He closed his eyes and waited . . .

She drew the steak knife from the drawer and tapped her finger on the tip. "Ow!" Sherry Coleton sucked the blood off and rinsed her hand under cold water. She laid the weapon on the counter beside her purse. Would it be wise to carry it? She asked herself. Would she be able to reach it in time if that demon child turned on her? One could only hope. The decision was made. The knife would stay with her whenever she left the house. She shut off the tap and examined her wounded finger. The injury was superficial and no longer bled, so she dried it off on a dish towel and dropped the blade into her handbag. William, Donald wasn't going to succeed in his family plan. If her own life had to end to stop him, then so be it. Child or not, he should've known better than to take a life. What had really happened in his childhood to bring such insanity into his undeveloped brain? He mentioned his father had done other things to him. What was meant by that, head games? Sexual abuse perhaps. Whatever the case, it was enough to push him to at least one murder and god knows what else. She checked her watch. School was out over a half an hour ago. Where **was** he? Maybe he went off and died somewhere. Unlikely, but wouldn't it be dandy to receive a call saying her son had been found. 'He was struck by a car' she could hear the officer say. 'So sorry for your loss.' It would take great willpower to resist shouting, 'Thank god, I've been waiting for this moment!' She would of course be looked upon as crazy and they'd haul her off to the psycho ward for an evaluation . . .

Alright, enough daydreaming. Henry would be home in a couple of hours and dinner would have to be on the stove. Chicken legs were thawed in the fridge overnight. Mashed spuds and mixed veggies would make a quick meal leaving her plenty of time to clean house. Yes, Donald's room was included. Keep him unsuspecting then spring the trap. Let's just hope it doesn't backfire. Who knows what the little shit is capable of.

It wasn't working, at least not as planned. This world looked more like a ghost town than a bustling western city. Not only were there no people, but all the buildings were decrepit and gloomy clouds hovered in the darkened sky. Where was the sunshine he pictured, and where were the people? Slowly he strolled toward the tavern. Might as well have a look around. The vision could be delayed slightly. Surely in a few moments, townsfolk would be scurrying about and if luck was with him, there'd be an old fashioned shoot out. He was almost on the porch when a noise caught his attention. It came from under the stoop. He bent down to have a closer look and tilted his head. Through the blackness nothing moved. A chill ran up his back and he nervously glanced around. This hadn't been part of the program. The scratching commenced as though an opossum or other such creature was digging out through the floor boards. Again he peeked into the dark and saw nothing. There was no point in searching any further. The game was over. He shut his eyes in an attempt to return to the park. Before he could open them to discover he hadn't flourished in his effort, a low, menacing growl erupted from behind. He spun to face whatever animal had materialized against his will and found himself face to face with a snow white wolf. It was sizing him up, licking its fangs and gurgling from its throat. His heart began to race and he stepped away. As he did it sat on its haunches. It was smiling at him. "Good doggie." He cooed as he continued to creep toward the tavern stairs. His hands he held out as a shield. The wolf stood and followed. Donald didn't judge the distance to the stairs as well as he hoped. He fell backward onto them when his heel struck the bottom step. Again the wolf sat, its fur glistening despite the lack of sun. He turned around to scramble for safety, but stopped short when the beast spoke. "Leaving so soon? I haven't introduced myself yet." Its voice was low and gravelly. Caught off guard, he crawled ahead to prop against the exterior tavern wall. The grainy wood scratched his back as he forced himself to his feet. Splinters flaked off and fell to the floor. Some caught his shirt on their way down, poking tiny holes through the fabric. His flesh itched wherever they touched and he scratched for relief. None came. "Doesn't feel good, does it?" The intimidating dog asked. "Now you know how it feels," "What on earth do you mean?" He whined as he wiggled to reach more of the irritation. His effort was in vain. He may as well have been rolling in fiberglass insulation. "If you want it to stop, then **you** must stop." The groan mixed with a whimper and trailed off. The animal began to transform. Its pearl coat darkened to a deep shade of grey before it stood erect. The fangs which were partially hidden by the lip, doubled in length and its irises turned blood red. Donald screamed when it moved closer and hid his face. "What do you want with me?" he yelled. He couldn't send it away despite his best effort. This was not his creation. Someone or something was manipulating it. Still, it had to be fantasy right? Soon he'd open his eyes and all would be normal. Perhaps he'd fallen asleep and sunk into a nightmare. Perhaps . . . "I want you to stop. If you wish to stay sane, do not come to these places. End it now." Donald put his hand over his eyes and peered toward the hallucination. He continued to stare through his fingers as it dropped to all fours and returned to its original form. "You've been warned." It said before trotting off. As it went, so did the imaginary surroundings and before he could blink, he was again in the park. The wood itch vaporized along with the architecture and as he dropped his arms, he breathed a sigh of relief. There'd be no returning to his getaway resorts for a while. Obviously there was something off with his creative ability. Something that needed to either to be explored or cast aside for the time being. He headed toward home and his imitation family. His business with them was likely the cause of the confusion in his psyche, but that didn't explain the strange wolf or bizarre warning it gave off. What was he telling himself to end, his vision quests? If so, for what gain? To better his relationship with people on **this** plain of existence? There was another answer. His mother or the power could be forcing him to choose between the two. Why though? What was wrong with enjoying the alone time he so badly needed? It wasn't as though he neglected those around him. If anything the escapes made dealing with real people and every day situations somewhat more tolerable. Whatever the case he had much soul searching to look forward to. He stormed from the wooded area toward the lush lawn of the lower park. Disappointed and discouraged he balled his fists and huffed. "Screw it." Bitterly he kicked a golf ball sized rock down the slope. "Screw it all."

Dinner was almost ready and night was falling. As usual William wasn't home yet, nor Henry. William, how trying it was to use that name. William . . . He was gone, replaced by a replica. Now every time she gazed into that vacant expression she could only think Donald. Home wrecker, manipulator, evil little prick. The front door squeaked on its hinges. Sherry knew who it was, not by voice but the slam. "I'm home mom. Is dad here yet?" She rushed to the foyer. Donald was already half way to the kitchen. Water footprints followed him. "Don, I mean William, why are you wearing your shoes indoors? Look at them, they're soaking wet and you're messing up the carpet. Take them off please." He looked down but showed no concern toward the mess. If anything he was amused by it. "Relax ma, it'll vacuum out when it dries. Lay a towel down or somethin'." His blatant disregard for her fired up frustration. Who cared what the twerp could do. He wasn't about to get away with such ignorance. "How dare you speak to me as if I'm your maid. Just because you're too lazy and self-righteous to lift a finger around here doesn't give you the right to deliberately mess the place. Now take off those damn shoes!" Donald was surprised. It was doubtful anyone had spoken to him so directly about his behavior, or at all for that matter. He stood unmoving. A dumbfounded gawk was his reply before he slowly kicked off the saturated runners. "Socks too." His eyes bugged in defiance and his lip curled, but he obeyed. "Thank you. Now wash up. Dad'll be home soon. Won't it be wonderful to eat together as a family Donald?" He was headed for the stairs when she caught him off guard. He stopped in his tracks but faced the door rather than her. This was the beginning. A nerve had been struck. "It's nice to have people care after so long, isn't it? Someone to give you something your real folks didn't." His shoulders heaved and he slowly turned her way. The child, who moments ago could show no emotion, was crying like a baby. "You,

you said Donald," he choked. "Not William . . ." Hands to face he stumbled forward. When he reached her, his arms opened and he wrapped them tightly around her waist. Tears drenched her blouse and she placed a hand over his shoulders and one on his head. No longer did she take comfort in the idea to discard him as before. No one she'd known had been as broken as he and she found herself accepting his dysfunction. For all she knew they were meant to find each other. Besides, if she had been subject to similar circumstances, she may have turned out no different. How could she judge him? Would you put down a family pet for scratching furniture? Yes he'd taken her son, but he'd also replaced him. The family may work after all, considering the boy was capable of emotion. 'Don't let him toy with you' kept repeating in the back of her mind. She ignored it as quickly as she'd forgiven. He was still sobbing when she knelt before him. Holding him at arms length she discovered he'd changed to his true form. "It's alright", she cooed. His chin came up but he kept his eyes down. "We're family now. I'm not perfect but I'll tell you this," Finally he made eye contact. "I'll do my best to be a good mother if you work with me. I'm done with fighting you and I want . . . No, I need you to help me instead of arguing or ignoring me. I don't ask for much and if you feel pressured, talk to me. It's what I'm here for." She pet his head and he grinned. "Of course I'll have to call you William when Henry's around." He chuckled, "Okay, I'll do my part." "There's a good boy." She stood. Relieved, she waved him on. "Wash up son, dinners nearly ready, and don't forget to dress as William." "Gotcha." He squealed as he raced up the stairs.

All three were quiet during dinner. Henry must've had a bad day. He wasn't usually so moody. When the meal was done William volunteered to clear the table, which raised some eyebrows. Henry spent his time with the television while mom and son giggled in the kitchen. The psychologist must've done something right during the meeting. Hopefully this was the beginning of a new chapter and William's behavior wouldn't reduce to isolation again. The news offered little entertainment so he shut the T.V. off. No use hearing how depressing the world had become with its violence and natural disasters. There were enough problems in the confines of the home to concern himself with, which was why there'd be another gathering once the kitchen was cleaned.

Though he could leave things as they were, he wasn't completely convinced the newly found co-operation was permanent. There were guidelines to be set, rules to be written and followed. Structure was the way to go to maintain solace and as father and husband, it was his duty to set the wheels in motion and monitor the progress. Strict discipline as he'd grown up with was the way to go. Don't spare the rod and spoil the child. Enough of that had already been done, hence William's rebellious ways. The laughing and joking continued in the kitchen. A cover to set his mind at ease? Possibly, but it would continue, he'd make sure.

"Would you like some tea dear?" Sherry offered. Henry shook his head. "Both of you come here. I've something I'd like to discuss." Donald and Sherry looked at each other with curiosity imprinted on their faces. Donald shrugged and strolled to the living room with mom on his heels. He took his place on the couch which he presently labeled the hot seat. What had Henry on his mind which was so important? Maybe a trip to Disneyland, but judging by the look he gave he was likely to announce a recent family death. When Sherry was seated, he began. "You two seem quite chipper this evening. I'd like to know what your counselor had to say." Oops, wrong on both counts. "You know; the usual." Sherry said with humility. "No, I don't know," Henry straightened himself in his recliner. Geez, talking with him was more of a drill session than conversation. Hopefully he wouldn't be too much of a downer. No need to spoil a good thing. "Please elaborate." "We can't." Donald cut in before Sherry could answer. "It's confidential." Right then he expected no support. Rather, he braced for a tongue lashing. Sherry shocked him by rising to his defense. "Yes, confidential. You know, like your job you never talk about. Don't worry yourself over us. We're working out our differences just fine." Henry raised his eyebrows. He'd been put in his place. It was a pleasant surprise to say the least. As stupefied as he was, he couldn't come up with a counter debate. The silence was heavenly while it lasted, but then he played his top card. "Well, regardless of the fact, as the man of the house I have some ground rules to establish to ensure your, uh, sorted differences remain resolved. Let's begin with consequences. William, you will be grounded for every chore you refuse. If that doesn't work, I'm sure we can find a more physical punishment. No more tardiness after school unless we've agreed on it, and you'll be visiting your counselor twice a week." "Now just a minute," Sherry snapped. Her face reddened as she defended her son. Perhaps she saw that Henry wasn't the good father he portrayed himself to be and his so-called disciplines were no more than stress creators. What had changed to cause him to react like an enforcer? It seems his gut feelings were right after all, but there was something more to it, something external. Sherry must've picked up on it as well. Her nervousness showed through by her defiant response. "I'm not letting you dictate how I raise my boy, and where do you get off playing father when you haven't even been a good husband?" He raised a finger and was about to speak but she stopped him cold. "I'm not done. As far as counseling goes, you either go with us or drop the subject now. Being as you'll be too busy with your time to make any appointments, we'll forget it was mentioned." He rolled his eyes. "Yeah, that's what I thought, and you're crazy if you think I'll allow physical punishment. What are you thinking? Are you trying to undo the progress we've made?" Henry stood red-faced and bitter. "Now you listen, bitch. I'm the head of the home and **I'll** decide what's best. Until you pay the bills, it's the way it's gonna be. William, go upstairs." Donald cringed against the chesterfield. A fear he'd forgotten reared up and he began to shake. Sherry gasped from disbelief. She swallowed hard before continuing. Donald noticed her hands also trembled. Was the thumping in his ears his heart or hers? "Well maybe I'm done with you and your bullying. Go spend the night at a hotel. I don't want you . . ." Henry pulled back and smashed Sherry's mouth with the back of his hand. A loud 'smack' bounced off the walls along with her shrill yelp. His knuckle tore her lip and blood droplets peppered Donald's cheek. He squeezed his eyes tight and began rocking. A hand grabbed his arm like a vise and yanked him to his feet. His leg hit the coffee table and he winced from the pain. "I said upstairs." Henry shoved him forward and he fell. On impact something in his frail mind shifted, removing any trace of fear and pain. He scrambled to his feet and faced off with Henry. From the corner of his eye he could see Sherry holding her hand over her mouth. Crimson drops seeped through her fingers and fell to her lap. Mommy was bleeding like before. It stained the edge of the diving board along with strands of ebony hair. Dad was at fault. Daddy had made him this way and he knew when it began. It was summer time and he was five. They were on a camping trip to Vancouver Island and dad promised to take him fishing. After traipsing through the woods for what felt like an hour, they came across a clearing. There was a cabin, a rundown shack with a sunken ceiling and rot holes in the floor boards. Moss covered a portion of the front wall and most of the roof. There was no stream, only one fishing rod with tangled line and a rusty hook. There would be no fishing after all. The memories were extremely vivid. So much so that he may have thought he was reliving it, had it not been for the absence of physical sensation. Dad took him inside and stripped him down. His imagination took over from that point on. He was no longer with his tormentor in the old wooden shack, but sailing high above a mountain ridge with a pair of bald eagles. Now and then he'd return to his torture as the agony jerked him to reality. Hours seemed to fly by and before long he was dressed and headed for the camp site. Mom never knew of the abuse. He should've told her. It could've stopped long before and he wouldn't have blamed her for being so blind. She would still be alive had he only released his secret. It was too late for that now, but not for his new mother. Vision flocculated as he released his deadly stare. Henry glared back triggering a flow of contempt and veins stood out on his arms and neck. There were many ways to end this power struggle, but death would not be one of them. No, Henry would learn his lesson by living with it the rest of his days. "Get to your room you little shit, before I beat the bark off you!" Donald clenched

*VISIONS*

his fists and stood his ground. Henry raised a hand and stepped forward. A wave of heat swept over the room and instantly he paused. As sweat poured off his forehead he glanced around as though looking for the source. "You'll never touch us again." Donald snarled. Something wet trickled from his nose and dripped to the carpet. The vessels in the whites of his eyes flashed in his vision with each beat of his heart. Though they throbbed painfully, he ignored them. His rage had reached full capacity and the power poured forth in a brilliant flash. Henry threw his hands over his face a split second before the unseen energy thrust him hard against the wall. A family photo fell to the floor and burst into flame. Sherry didn't move. Frozen in time, she was not permitted to witness anymore violence. It was the only way to protect her from further harm. The power kept pressure on Henry as he remained pressed against the damaged wall. It would not release him until Donald's blood lust subsided . . . The room began to dim as anger slowly slipped away. Donald fell to his knees exhausted. Briefly he hung there, limp and drained, before collapsing to the carpet.

It was dark. The house bore an unsettling silence. Donald raised his head and scanned the room. Sherry lay on the couch. Her chest rose and fell with each breath. She was sleeping. So was Henry. Face down he lay, arms to his sides. The burned picture which used to show him with Sherry and William lay by his head in a charred mess. The wall showed no signs of damage, nor did Sherry's face. It was as though the incident hadn't happened. Slowly he forced himself to stand and hobble to the light switch. His leg had a heavy bruise where it struck the table. It was already purple and swollen. Why it hadn't healed was a mystery he was content not to explore. He flicked the switch and light flooded the room, chasing away twisted shadows. Sherry opened her eyes. Slowly she propped herself on an elbow then pushed herself upright. Donald didn't so much as twitch, but studied her movements. She put her hand to her lip then pulled it away to examine it. "No blood." She said slightly above a whisper. When she spotted Henry unconscious on the floor she turned to him. "Donald, what happened? Is he dead?" Her answer came in the form of a soft grunt. Henry would be sleeping a while yet. He went to her and sat down. "He'll be fine, so will you." He wrapped heavy arms around her and buried his head in her bosom. "We'll all be okay now." "What did you do Donald? Tell me, I need to know." He raised his head and stared into her sorrowful eyes. "I stopped him. He won't bother us again." The power had saved them. When he thought it was lost for good, it returned in his hour of need. It was all he needed to know. As the hand of God had struck Saul, so the power which protected him had done with Henry. When he came to he would be a changed man, whether he wanted it or not. For almost an hour they held each other. Mother and son who no man could separate. Henry groaned and rolled over. "He's waking. Are you going to disguise yourself?" Donald ran his hand down the bridge of his nose. He hadn't noticed the transformation. "No" he said with a hint of contentment. "There'll be no need, you'll see." They watched as Henry pushed himself to his hands and knees. His hands groped ahead of him for something to use as a prop. He swiveled right until he found the coffee table. Once he held it in both hands he called out. "Anyone here?"

Sherry put her hands to her mouth and gasped as he raised his head. His corneas were milky white. Henry had been struck blind. "Yeah, Henry." Donald sneered,

"We're both here." "Help me," he begged. "Your recliner's to your right. Have a seat. We'll call you an ambulance." Inquisitively, Henry asked, "Who are you boy? Whose with you?" "**I'm** here." Sherry chimed. "Your wife . . ." Donald put a finger to his lip and she fell silent. He whispered in her ear. "He's not your husband, not anymore. I've changed that. This is your way out if you want it. Don't worry about money. His account is in your name. You can start over." Her eyes widened. "You . . . you did this for **me**?" "Yes," He smiled and brushed her cheek. "If you want it. Tell me before I dial the authorities. Is it what you want?" Tears dripped from the corner of her eyes and rolled down her cheek. Not tears of loss or sadness, but of joy at the chance of correcting the biggest mistake of her life. There'd been no real happiness in the marriage. Only during the honeymoon and William's birth did she feel she'd accomplished anything important. All the years of existing in the stagnant home with synthetic love had calloused her soul and she'd become almost as numb as Henry. Never in her wildest imagination had she expected a violent outburst, let alone being struck. Whatever the reason was for his behavioral change, she was grateful it was over, permanently. Ironic how it took a boy she hardly knew to bring to light her vain existence. Yes, he had the uncanny knack of bringing out the best and worst in people. And here was her chance to start anew with a son who could fulfill her every wish, even though he already had. She was free for the first time in over ten years and Donald, the child she wished for dead had performed the miracle. "Yes." She nodded with great enthusiasm. "It **is** what I want. Thank you." She squeezed him tight but he didn't mind. He'd given her what he couldn't give his other mom. Hope. "Okay you can let go now." He looked at Henry who was mumbling and waving his fingers over his face. "I've got a call to make."

By midnight the ambulance holding Henry was on its way to the hospital. Donald and Sherry stood side by side in a downpour as it vanished around the bend. Donald looked to his bare feet. The rain tickled as it bounced off them and the surrounding concrete. It wasn't cold as he expected, rather lukewarm as the driveway asphalt and soothing as a message only nature could master. The rest of him was soaked. So was new mom. Her hair hung straight down the sides of her head, stringy and much darker than the usual deep amber with soft gold highlights. In the dim light she appeared younger, as though ten years of stress had washed away. Indeed it must have. "Come, I'll make us hot chocolate." She led him into the house. While she stripped off her coat he headed for the bathroom linen closet. When he came out she was already in the kitchen. "Here," he said, distracting her from the stove top. He handed her a towel. "Dry your hair." "Thanks Donald, that was sweet." He took a seat at the table and watched her wrap the towel over her head. "Mom?" he asked, "Do you think you'll be wanting another husband? Not right away, but ever?" She filled the kettle and dug two packets of cocoa from the cupboard. She hardly seemed distracted by the query. "Oh, I don't know. Maybe one day. I'd like to enjoy single life for a while." After turning the element to high, she joined him. "Why do you ask?" "Oh, I don't know, I guess I'm tired of father figures. They don't treat me right. Not like mom, not like you."

After sipping their drinks and chatting over cream-filled and chocolate chip cookies, they said goodnight and headed to their rooms. Around three, Donald bolted up in bed. He didn't feel right. At first he though the bed-time snacks were the culprit and the reason for the night terrors that plagued his once pleasant dreams. It was more than that. Everyone he'd hurt had come back to haunt him. William, Jaden, they were there along with mom and dad. Not Henry though. Somehow he remained at bay; probably because he was the only one of the five still breathing. His head ached as well as his tummy. A cold presence seemed to loom overhead as though planning punishment for his crimes against humanity. His heart palpitated and his hands trembled. Slowly he dragged himself from bed and staggered to the hall, the sense of impending doom growing ever more prevalent. Paranoia began to set in as images of his victims consumed his thoughts. They wanted justice. He pictured them treating him the same as he'd done to them. Was it his own conscience plaguing his emotion or were they really coming forth to collect their dues? It hurt to think of it. His stomach churned and he hastened his pace to the washroom.

Sherry rolled over and opened her eyes. A thump in the hall had awakened her. Laying still she cocked an ear and waited. A bump off the bathroom wall prompted her to sit up. She knew it was Donald making the noise and would've left things be, but that motherly instinct insisted something unusual was taking place. He might be sick. After all, he ate seven cookies in one sitting. Not many children could handle **that** before bed. The water tap went on and she could tell by the trickle he was running his fingers through the spray. A frog like croak came from him and it was obvious he was gagging. She stood and wrapped her housecoat over her pajamas. She had no time to tie the waste belt when a horrible crash echoed through the thin walls. "Oh my god," she gasped.

Quickly as possible she scurried to the open bathroom door and looked inside. On the floor, knees to his chest lay Donald. With hands folded over his stomach, he lay on his side shivering. As sweat poured from his face, his features changed as though deciding William's or his own identity. Flesh rippled as a snake shedding skin and blood trickled from his nostrils. His hair debated which was its true colour and length. Thin, dark and an inch long as Donald's or lighter, fuller and a couple inches longer as William's. The shivers became tremors and his whole body convulsed and jerked. "Help . . . me," he managed to plea through shallow gasps. She rushed to his side but dared not touch him. His body was in a state of flux and there was no telling what would happen if contact was made. "Hold on son, you'll be fine." If she could believe it herself she might sound more convincing. In the tub was a face cloth. She retrieved it and rinsed it under the cold tap. If she could cool him down, it may ease the symptoms. After folding it in two, she held it above his forehead and gently lowered it before letting it go. It dropped into place. His body stopped quaking and went rigid. Every muscle strained and stiffened, though the flocculation receded and ceased. He was on his back staring wildly at the ceiling. She reached for him hoping the worst was over and touched his arm . . .

He was scarcely aware of anything around him. What was **in** him was altogether different. Every vision, every quest and teleportation he'd gone through flipped in his head like a picture book. It was like dreaming them over and over, one right after the other. He'd taken the place of his victims and endured the horror he'd put them through again and again. He wanted to cry, to call out to mommy to hold him and make things better, but she wouldn't come.

His appeal would be ignored with the same calculating coldness he'd shown to William and Jaden. The wolf had returned. Over and over it repeated, 'if you want to be sane, do not come to these places. Stop now.' It wouldn't hold one shape, but contorted back and forth from white small wolf to menacing grey judge advocate. He may as well been on a satanic roller coaster, for his senses surged with adrenaline as his mind was yanked to and fro. There was nothing to do but ride it out and hope it would soon end. Something warm touched his arm. At first it was soothing and a welcome change, but as quickly as it comforted it began to burn. Claws dug in, penetrating to the bone. They tightened, crushing and grinding his forearm to mush. It must be pay back for what he'd done to Jaden. As pressure built, he tried desperately to ignore the trauma. The intense anguish won out, flooding his head with a blood curdling scream. Then all was dark.

As soon as her fingers fell on his flesh, Donald let loose an ear piercing squeal. She pulled away but it was too late. His eyes shut and he lay limp. The urge to hold him was great. At the moment she didn't know whether he was alive or dead. Defeated, she lay against the cupboard, legs sprawled beside him. Ruby streams trickled down his cheeks to the floor, forming small puddles. She could do nothing about it. As close as he was, he was equally far away. Whatever gave him the ability to do as he did, had somehow turned against him. There was nothing to do but hope and pray he'd come out of it with no side effects. Folding her hands, she laid them on her lap. Never had she been so hopeless and alone.

At eight-thirty a.m. Sherry plopped herself down at the kitchen table with a steaming cup of chi tea. After sitting up most of the early morning with Donald, she'd had enough. Obviously he wasn't waking up anytime soon, so she dragged him to the hallway and carried him to bed. Yes, she understood her touch may do him harm. Why else would she wait until seven to move him? On the linoleum he was out of place and likely, if he felt anything at all, uncomfortable. He'd be much happier to arise on a soft warm mattress. Mentally and physically drained, she sipped from the cup as she cradled it between her hands. The porcelain was hot but not enough to burn, only disperse the cold chills of the vacant home. Vacant home, empty soul. What good was it to live this way?

Live? Hardly. Mere existence is what life had come to, which was no better than before Donald's arrival. Why had he come to **her**? Out of the millions of people who could provide a decent environment with love and acceptance, he'd chosen a naive woman and deceptive man as caretakers. With no major bond with her birth child she was a poor option at best, yet something brought them together. Since his arrival into their mundane and all too routine schedule a change had developed. Through distrust born of his early behavior, she had awaken and become aware of subtle changes in who she thought was her son. If not for the alterations, her perception would've stayed as is and she'd have been numb and dull forever. Despite it all, through some kind of miracle they'd found each other. A wake up call from God? If so, why was he taking her new child away? Perhaps he had something to do with Henry's odd behavior. Or maybe **she** had pushed him to snap with her unwarranted judgments. No, though things seemed fine until Donald appeared on the scene, she'd really been dealing with mild depression due to loneliness. She hadn't taken time to know her husband, which may have contributed to his repressed anger. Strange how she hadn't been able to see it before. No sense dwelling on it now. She was finally content with just herself and Donald. Free from previous poor choices and unfortunate circumstances. Unless misery was destined to plague them, he should soon come around. Maybe rest was all that was needed. Maybe this was his way of regenerating. Maybe it would be best not to jump to conclusions and patiently wait. She set the cup down. There were chores to be done. The bathroom is where she'd start. Dried blood from the floor and sink would be first. The cloth she used to mop his face needed rinsing and . . . Wait a minute. William had a microscope in his room that he rarely used. She could examine Donald's blood. To what end she had no idea, but a quick comparison with hers might show something out of the ordinary. What she hoped to find eluded her. A difference in colour, clarity, cell size? Something may stand out and prove what? That his DNA may not be human? Yes, there was that possibility and knowing would be better than not. Suppose it was, would she love him any more or less? He was still who he was and nothing would change that. Questioning that choice was futile at best, for she knew deep down the love was unconditional. Enough rationalizing. Time to put thought to action. She headed for the stairs. She was about to grab the handrail and begin the climb when the phone rang in the kitchen. Fighting disappointment, she huffed and rushed to it. "Hello?" Mrs. Hemmingway answered back. "Hi, Mrs. Coleton, this is William's teacher." "Yes, I know your voice." She hissed, aware of how bitchy she must've come across. "Donald won't be . . . I mean William is home sick. He should be back to class Monday." "Yes, thank you but that's not the only reason I called. I have some art pictures William drew. They're quite good."

Sherry sighed with frustration. Not wishing to be hostile she took a deep breath before she continued. "That's great Mrs. Hemmingway." She said with little enthusiasm. "I'll come in later to look at them, but I'm preoccupied at the moment." "Please do." Sherry caught a hint of distress. "It's best you see them for yourself. Can you make it here between three and four today?" "Yes, I'll certainly try, thank you." She hung up without allowing Hemmingway to say goodbye. With the distractions in the home she had little concern for art pictures. Still she'd keep the appointment if for nothing more than to satisfy teacher. To the staircase she rushed, the caffeine ever gradually increasing her energy level and anxiety.

The microscope lay on the closet floor under a stack of comics and clothes. Still in the box, she wondered if William had used it at all. Once in hand she turned her focus on Donald. Though his chest rose and fell with each breath, his pale skin and shadows gave him a deathly appearance. She bent down and kissed his forehead. It was warm. "Wake up soon." She softly whispered. "I miss you."

Once downstairs she bee lined for the bathroom and hit the light switch. At the counter she pried open one end of the box and slid out the Styrofoam tray and its contents. Three glass slides lay in makeshift slots. She removed two and set them side by side on the counter before setting up the scope. After adjusting the reflective mirror for maximum lighting she searched for a pin to prick her finger. She found one in the bottom of the left drawer underneath a bar of generic soap. Once used to pop boils, it had been stowed after William's breakouts ceased. He was four then and for nearly a month, pus filled pockets broke out on his backside. Almost daily she would have to drain and disinfect them, and boy did he shriek when the pin came out. Luckily he had few treatments, which was in itself a great relief for them both. After, he stayed clear whenever she hemmed pant legs or hand sewed any clothing that needed mending. She chuckled at the mental picture, but her grin faded as past made way for the present and her task at hand. Using the tip, she scraped a miniscule amount of Donald's diluted fluid from the sink and dripped it onto one slide. When satisfied there was plenty, she carefully positioned it on to the microscope. She then turned on the tap and collected a drop of water to mix with her sample. The comparison had to be fair. With no hesitation she jabbed the end of her finger. She winced from the prick and set the pin down. Over the slide she held her finger and squeezed until a drop fell. The water immediately thinned and spread it over the glass. Sample two complete. Over the microscope eye piece she hovered. Did she really need to know what was out of her hands? "He's still my son." She whispered to the walls. "I'll still love him, I will." Though convinced she remained hesitant, but she fought through it and placed her eye over the lens. Blood cells could clearly be seen, though fuzzy around the edges. She used the control knob below the eye piece to bring it to clarity. Nothing seemed amiss other than small reflective flecks in the mix. They sparkled with multiple rainbow colours as diamonds. "Must be the water molecules," she muttered before pulling back. Her specimen may be no different. Once in place she peered at it and made mental notes of the similarities. One element was off. Her blood contained none of the sparkly flecks his had. She knew without question they must some how contribute to his telekinetic ability. At least her anxieties were put to rest.

He was human after all. "Mom . . ." The weak cry wafted to her ears as though riding on a gentle breeze. The experiment was over. Time to switch from scientist to mother. She climbed the stairs two at a time and marveled at the thought she too had the ability to change.

"How do you feel? You getting hungry?" Donald nodded and sat up. "Starving, could you order pizza?" "Really?" Sherry cocked her head and stared inquisitively. "Yes, please, if you don't mind. You can pay with Henry's debit card. I saw it downstairs on the recliner. The p.i.n. number is five, three, seven, five." She frowned with the need to know how he could possibly have figured out the p.i.n., but chose to shrug it off. Some things just didn't matter. "Okay then, pizza it is, anything else?" "Yes." He threw his legs over the edge of the bed and stretched his arms, then wrapped them around her. "I love you."

Within the hour the delivery driver was at the door. Sherry, debit card in hand, followed him back to the car. Donald had written the number down for her, which she glanced at before typing in. As she pressed the keypad she memorized the letters for each number to see if they'd spell anything. When she pressed enter she laughed. How ironic for the letters to spell j.e.r.k. The driver handed back the card along with the two medium specials. After thanking him she headed into the house, still giggling. "It's the card number, isn't it?" Donald asked. "That's why you're laughing." "Yeah, how do you know?" She set the boxes on the table. Donald carelessly popped the top and grabbed a slice. "I changed it." He said with a smirk. "I wanted something simple so you'd remember it." He stuffed the pointed end into his mouth and bit the slice in half. How he avoided choking was anyone's guess. Sherry went to the fridge and selected a fresh carton of apple juice. After removing the foil tab from the spout, she poured him and herself a glass. "I must say young man, you have quite a creative touch. Speaking of which, I've been asked to review some of your school work today. I have an appointment with your teacher in . . ." she strained for a better view of the stove clock. Two-thirty already; where'd the time go? "Wow, in less than an hour. Will you be fine by yourself?" She helped herself to the pizza. "Sure I will." "Good. The run of the house is yours. Please don't let anyone in. Don't even answer the door." "I won't mom," he promised.

Mrs. Hemmingway was behind her desk reading over some student papers when she entered the room. "Ah, Mrs. Coleton, glad you could make it." "Hi, Mrs. Hemmingway, call me Sherry." "Alright Sherry and please, call me Fiona. Have a seat." She pointed at the desk across from hers. Sherry pulled the chair out from under it and sat down. It was small but not uncomfortable, despite her knees being too close to her chest. She straightened her legs beneath the desk and brushed wrinkles from her slacks. As a youth she had spent years in these seats. Hard to believe grade five to seven were spent in this very school, her first class being one room over. "I don't recall the desks being this low." She jested. "Mind you, it's been a while." Fiona ignored her as she shuffled through a stack of papers. She found Donald's drawings and brought them over. After dropping them under Sherry's nose she slid a chair over from the opposing desk. "Take a good look," she said as she leaned close. "And tell me if you recognize the man in this first one." Sherry carefully examined the drawing. Immediately it was clear who the gentleman was, but doubtful Donald perceived him in that way. Judging by the tears on his face, this was his old home and the man was dad. "No, I haven't seen him before." The pencil strokes were intricate, almost as though he'd used charcoal for the shadows. This was the work of a genius, not a child. "My god, they're wonderful. Such amazing detail. How long did it take to draw these?" "Would you believe less than two hours?" Sherry's jaw dropped. "Yeah, I was shocked as well. Take a look in the bottom right corner. What do you see?" Through the array of fine lines and smudges she searched but could see nothing. "Look for something out of the ordinary like you would if you were comparing a counterfeit bill to a real one." That would be easy had she another copy to compare it to. Her eyes ached from strain. Through the clutter, a word suddenly popped out. She remembered the brain teasers in the Sunday paper. Unlike this, she couldn't nor ever did find a hidden portrait in them. "It says 'past', is that right?" Fiona nodded. "And check the same area on the next two." They were much easier to spot. "Hmm, present and . . . future? The drawing of the present had been dated, unlike the others. 1983 was printed in the lower right hand corner. What do you suppose it means?" Fiona shrugged. "Beats me, but if this is how he pictures his own life, I'd be concerned." She had a right to be so. Whatever the boy on the second page represented wasn't good. If it was Donald, it could resemble hopelessness as his life spiraled into a pit of despair. Mind you, he wasn't that way lately. His outlook may have changed. His future was no brighter. What type of room was he in, a chemistry lab? He was horrified. Was this still to come or had his behavioral changes rerouted his future? Or maybe in his sleep he had merely dreamt it all. "I wouldn't be worried. He did have some problems this week but they've been resolved. May I take these?" "Of course you can. I've already graded them. He got an 'A.'"

Sherry beamed. "I knew he was smart, but talented? I'm pleasantly surprised." "Me too, well, that's it. We're done here unless you have any other concerns." Sherry shook her head. "No, and thanks for recommending Mr. Kueber. He was most helpful." "Anytime." The women said their goodbyes and Sherry headed out. Fiona looked on with a troubled frown. Things may be better for now, but no one changes that drastically overnight. No one.

"Donald, are you here?" Sherry pushed her way in, keys in one hand and Donald's art in the other. She was pleased with him. So pleased that she would have to reward him for his fabulous work. As she kicked her shoes off, he appeared in the hall. "There you are my wonderful little man. I have good news for you." "What is it?" he asked, pleased to see her in such a fine mood. "I just came from your school as you know, and I'm happy to say you've earned your first 'A'. And because you have impressed me so, name something you want and I'll make sure you get it." His face fell. "Can you find me a way to go back to school as your son?" He turned away and dragged himself toward the living room. "What on earth do you mean?" she enquired as she followed. He dropped onto the sofa and she perched at his side. He didn't respond right away. "What is it hon? What's bothering you?" He folded his hands and laid his elbows on his knees. "It's over." He mumbled as he stared at the floor. She gently rested her hand on his shoulder. "What's over?" "The power, it's gone." "Gone? How?" "I don't know. I tried to change back to William and I couldn't. I'm stuck this way. How can I go to school now?" She put her arm around his shoulder. "We'll find a way. I can adopt you. You can be yourself and I can still be your mother. Don't worry." She put her free hand on his art work which she'd set on the coffee table.

"In the meantime, I want you to be proud of yourself. I know **I** am. Recognize these?" She spread the three sheets out. To her surprise he backed away. "Easy," she softly said. "You're not in trouble. This is how you earned your 'A'. Honestly I haven't known anyone who could draw so well. I do have a question though, what do they represent?" She pushed the first drawing over, the one of the man with the beer bottle. He quickly glanced at it then turned away. "That's my dad." He mumbled, "And that's me behind the door. I lived in that shack before I came here." Her theory had been accurate. "Is that why you labeled it 'past'?" His head jerked up. His astonishment startled her. "I didn't label anything. That **is** my past, and if you don't mind, I'd like to forget it." He threw his arms across his chest and slumped against the backrest. "You **did** label it." She insisted. "You labeled the others too. Here, see for yourself." She placed the other two drawings over the first. "Come on, humor me. Right here and here, see? Present and future." Reluctantly he leaned forward and instantly he spotted the labels. "I don't get it. I don't recall drawing that in." "It doesn't matter now," she soothed. "What I'd like to know is if you still feel hopeless like **this** guy?" She pointed to Jaden. He'd completely forgotten about him. As he stared at the page, the realization of that day flooded in. How proud he was to have full control. There was still no remorse over what he'd done. He'd ridden the world not of a kid, but of a bully who was completely useless in society. Would he have grown to be a better man? Doubtful. Maybe a violent and bitter subnormal human, like his father. A parasite to whoever he came into contact with, but a better man, no way. "That isn't me," he said through gritted teeth. Anger began to fester. "He's the ass who bullied your son. I sent him away when he tried it with me. No one will miss him. In fact I'm the only one who knew he ever existed. I erased his memory as well as his life. He was useless anyway." Sherry grimaced in abject horror. She could scarcely believe what he was saying. How many more victims were there? He was smirking. How could he be proud of what he'd done? "Sorry if I'm scaring you. I'm sure you understand I did what I had to. I simply sent him away like Henry." "Not like Henry," she said as she slid to the edge of the couch. "He's still alive. My lord, that means you didn't need to kill William. You could've sent him away instead. I could've . . ." "Relax Sherry, who says he's dead? That's your assumption. I sent his body away, that's all. The rest of him, like his soul for example, could be anywhere. Like I said, he's likely in heaven. Jaden, well he could've gone either way. I'm sure wherever he is he's getting what he deserves. We all have to pay for our misdeeds, Mrs. Coleton. Don't you agree?" With hesitance, she brought herself to nod. The way his gaze seemed to burn right through to her spirit caused her to wonder what punishment he may be scheming for her. Thank god his powers were history or she could one day be facing his perverted form of justice as well. "And what punishment will **you** serve for your crimes? You don't expect to get off the hook, do you?" "Crimes?" he mocked. "I haven't committed any crimes." His voice rose and he stood. A malevolent force shaded the sparkle in his once happy glow and he stood above with fists clenched at his sides. "Was it a crime to kill a man who raped me from age five?" he shouted. "Did I deserve it? I should be given a metal!" He lowered his voice and ground his teeth. "My mother didn't protect me . . ." As he hesitated, Sherry noticed a change. It was slight but noticeable none the less. His personality shifted to another. Somehow change in mood determined whether or not he had any empathy. One minute it was there, the next completely wiped away. The instability was a sure sign that even **she** wasn't safe, no matter what he claimed. Any moment he could change his mind and send her away too. His extraordinary gift had returned to him, she was sure. He didn't seem aware or just didn't care at the moment, but she saw it plain as day when the flesh on his arms rippled. Determined to show no fear she kept her stare locked with his. Occasionally he'd look away, but when he glanced over again, her eyes were there to meet his. "I killed her because of him. I did. She didn't know. How could she? She was too busy setting up camp or doing chores. I never told her." His voice trembled in a whisper. "How could I? How could I break her heart? My own mother. My mom . . ." He wiped a tear from his reddened cheek. It was easy to feel sorry for him. So easy to relate to his sorrow. The poor child who suffered through what no human should endure deserved to finally be heard. He hadn't told a soul, it was obvious. For seven years he'd held in his terrible secret, but no more. At long last it would be fully revealed and she'd be the only one to know. Now it would be **their** secret and her responsibility to keep it. Again his expression soured. "It was an accident. I didn't want her to die." His upper lip curled. With a cold apathetic tone he poured out his plight. "She was supposed to fall in the water. I couldn't control it, it just came out. It wasn't my fault. She should've let me swim. She never let me have fun. It was either too dangerous or put off. 'Another time', she always said. What's wrong with right now mom? Why can't I swim? Because dad said so?" The words were forced out with each breath. His face grew a deeper shade of red with each passing second. His breathing was heavy and a twitch came to his left eye. "Don't listen to him mom, he's a liar. A god damn liar! Why did you heed his every word? You deserve what you got, bitch . . . no, no. I didn't mean that. I'm sorry mom. I'm always sorry . . ." He collapsed to the couch and held his head his hands. He wasn't weeping or panting like before. She touched his shoulder. "Don't." He whispered. "I don't deserve your sympathy. I don't deserve you. You're right. I'll be punished for what I've done. I already am. No more school, no more identity. I'm back to the beginning. As much as I tried I couldn't change a thing. I'm the same boy I was when I left home. When I wonder . . ." He turned his head. Hollow eyes glistened from the tear drops forming. "When will it let me go? When will I be free?" The streaks on his cheeks glistened like diamonds, reminding Sherry of the chemical compound in his blood sample. It could be purging itself from his system. Gently she gathered a drop on her finger before it could fall to the floor. It immediately it solidified. Carefully she broke it free with her thumb and forefinger, like snapping an icicle off a steel rail. It dropped to her palm. "I don't understand. Donald, what is this?" She held the glassy bead out for him to see. "The power." He simply replied. "It's leaving, I can tell. Keep it, there'll be no more. No more crying, no more mom and dad. No more anything for Donald. I should never have been born. I've been nothing but a disappointment." "Don't say things like that. I won't leave you, not ever." "No," he countered. "Probably not, but one day I'll leave **you.** We can't change who we are." Sherry closed her fingers over the tear drop and stared out the window. The sun had broken through the clouds and settled across the neighborhood. The window frame cast its shadow along the floor. Brilliant patches of sunlight stretched toward them. She pondered

Donald's words. No more crying. Not from her son or the sky. A new beginning was at hand. Whether Donald would be a part of it was undetermined. Without a thought she set the crystal gem on the table and reached for her boy. He didn't resist, but embraced her as the sunbeams crawled over and rested at their feet. "I want you to cherish this moment." She said. "Whenever you're sad or hurting remember I am your mother and I love you. You'll always be my Donald, no matter what. We may not be able to change who we are, but we can change who we become. As long as you believe it, there is still hope." They held each other until the sun set over the neighboring homes. The remainder of the evening was spent as any normal family would spend it. Donald played his first game of Uno and fell in love with it. Sherry made cocoa and pizza pops for dinner which they snacked on while they played into the night. At last Donald's bladder began to ache and he used the downstairs facility to relieve himself. When he came back to the table he had a curious expression. "What's on your mind, young man?" Sherry piped. She'd forgotten to clean the bathroom. His expression was a reminder. "You've been studying me. I saw the microscope. Why were you comparing our blood?" She froze. How could she explain her need to know without triggering a tantrum? After a quick deliberation she decided the truth was the best way to go. "I'm sorry. I wanted to be sure. I mean, I had to know you were . . ." "Human?" he smiled as he asked. "You weren't let down, were you?" She sighed with relief. "No, not at all. I was just curious." "And what was the result of your study?" She was nervous and he sensed it. "Relax I'd like to know for myself. Was my blood any different?" "Not really, just a little." "Tell me how. It was the crystals, right? The ones like in my tear?" She nodded. "Yes. Is that the reason for your gift, those tiny crystals?" "What do **you** think?" She grinned and nodded again. She couldn't shake her anxiety as though she unveiled a deadly secret she had no business knowing. One question still gnawed at her. Rather than second guessing herself, she spat it out. "How long have you had them? How long have you known they were there?" Okay, it was two questions, or rather the same one asked two different ways. Regardless there was but one answer. "Before mom died. Sometime that year, I think. It could've been just before. Don't ask how it came to be or why. Some things are better left unknown. I know you want to know how far I've pushed its limits. I can see it on your face." "Yes." She agreed. "If you're willing to fill me in, I'd like to hear it." "Alright then." He slid into his seat and set his elbows on the table. Her nervousness had abated somewhat. He hated her restlessness. Every time he sensed her fear the desire to lash out burned in his gut. What was worse was having to fight against it. It was far too easy to give in and normally he would, but the affection she'd shown had made her special. 'Don't fear me.' He wished to tell her. 'It only angers me.' He may have said something had he not understood that a dominant stance would antagonize the issue. He would leave things be. "Okay, I'll start from the beginning. As you know dad was cruel. Every night before bed I'd wish him dead. He used to punch me for no reason, but only when we were alone. Why he didn't hit mom I'll never know. Anyway, I used to get furious and hope one day I could kick his ass, I mean butt." Sherry smiled with approval. His mannerisms were becoming more civil. Finally he was aware and willing to change. "Shortly after, I began hearing voices. I thought at first it was my own conscience because it would tell me to be patient, to forgive him. It was the right thing to do even though I had to suffer because of it, so I chose to wait. Well, it wasn't long after that when we went to the neighbors for a barbeque. That was the day mom wouldn't let me swim. I felt so mistreated because it was dad who told her not to let me. I hated that she listened to him and wouldn't hear me out. She said she loved, me, but I guess she loved him more." He hesitated as though reliving the events and stared over her shoulder. How he described the events painted a vivid picture in the mind. She had known such atrocities only in nightmares and could scarcely imagine living with the damage induced by that terrible life style. There was no love, only survival. How he made it this far was truly remarkable. He pulled himself away from the daydream and refocused. "I wanted to push her in the pool is all," he said without missing a beat. "Just a shove to get her attention, but it all went wrong. I guess I was too angry. I didn't need to touch her. I didn't come close. Just a small shove to knock her to her knees and let her know I mattered. Instead it jumped from me as though I had gotten up and shoved her myself. I remember thinking I hated her. I shouldn't have, but I was too upset. I knew when her head hit the diving board it was over. The voice said so. It's been with me off and on ever since. When I killed dad I was scared at first. I didn't want what happened to mom to happen to him. People couldn't know I was a killer. Dad knew, that's why he locked me up and starved me. I was in that room for years. He came at me one evening. You see, there was an old man who used to climb on our shack above my room. I don't know why, but I think he slept up there some nights. It was weird. Dad called him my buddy. Well I guess that night he whacked the antenna and scrambled the TV reception. Dad went after him and chased him down the street before coming after me. Like I said, I was scared but I heard the voice again say it was time for payback. I'll never forget how strong I was then, as though I could take on the world. I ended up ripping the door off the hinges with a mere thought and knocked him over with it. The rest is too gross to describe. Let's just say there was a beer bottle involved. He died and I transported here." "Transported?" Wow, this was too weird to conceive. "How do you mean?" He grinned from ear to ear. "One thought," he said with a hint of arrogance. "That's all it took to come here, that's all it takes to use the power. It's that simple. The rest you know. As for how far I've pushed, well let's say I've been to some interesting places. Places I've created in my mind. I created them, therefore they exist and I could go there any time I wanted. Maybe not now, but whenever I needed to be alone, there I'd go. I have erased people's minds. I suppose the greatest thing I've done is erase Jaden. He still resides somewhere in this world or the next, but there's no proof he was born at all. I'm proud of myself for that. Well there it is. Now you know my life. You know, I feel so much better now that . . ." He froze and cocked an ear as though listening to something. "Can you hear that?" His voice became unsteady. "No Donald I can't." He bit his lower lip. Whatever it was had him worried. "What do you hear?" "They're calling me, like in my nightmare. They're accusing me of taking them from their loved ones. Can't you hear them? They're getting so loud." He covered his ears and tried blocking the accusations. What started out as whispers had grown into full blown shouts. As unbearable as they were, a more menacing tone overrode all. With each eruption of its scolding blame he cringed tighter and tighter until he thought he'd implode. "I warned you . . ." It sneered with a gravel grinding rumble that shook his inner core and pounded his scrambled brain. The wolf had him. He'd ignored it, choosing instead to continue with the abuse of power. He had to. There was no other method to confront his phobias. Isn't that why the power came to him in the first place? It tricked him. Why didn't it let him know long before there'd be consequences for the privilege of its protection? Doubtful it would have made much difference, but he'd have had a choice. Instead he was left with nothing to give back but his life. "Mom help, it hurts!" he begged, though he knew she couldn't help if she tried. "Hold on, it'll be okay." The faint reply came through. "That's right." The wolf scoffed. "It's almost over." His flesh tingled and began to warm. He slid from the chair and landed with a thud on the linoleum. Visions of his indiscretions continued to plague him to the extent he could no longer see the kitchen when his dry eyes opened. There was in its place, the faces of those he'd brought to his own form of justice. He opened his mouth but could not speak. No screams, not even a whisper, only faint gurgles that faded into the black.

When he fell from the chair, Sherry rushed to his side. His flesh bubbled and spit like the surface of boiling water. Minute translucent particles wisped over him in a fine mist. His D.N.A. was unraveling, his atoms flying apart layer by layer. "Donald!" She cried. Desperate to hold him she reached out, but found only empty space. A thin film of condensation coated her hand as the remains of his broken body wafted over her and dispersed into the air. Donald was gone. On her knees, she collapsed to her face where he lay moments before. The floor was damp. "No . . ." she whimpered. "Please, no . . ." Salty drops fell at the realization of her situation. She had lost her family. William, Henry and now Donald had left her alone. What had she done to deserve this torment? How could she go on knowing everything she once loved had been taken? Pounding her fists on her knees she raised her head and screamed, then hung it low as thoughts of suicide rushed in. Taking her life would be elementary. Park the car in the garage and run a hose through the window from the tailpipe. So easy . . . "We can change who we become." The soft echo chimed. It was her own words returning to her. What she had told Donald to induce comfort now did the same for her. "As long as you believe, there is still hope . . ." She could not easily dismiss her own logic. Perhaps it was Donald's way of saying goodbye. His final best wish given for her benefit. Maybe all he wanted was for her to retain memories of their life together. Maybe, just maybe, wherever he was he was doing the same. "Thank you," she whispered. "I'll always love you, my son." A scraping sound came from the living room as though something had brushed along the window pane. Wiping her swollen eyes she rushed over to see who or what had caused it. She nearly banged her leg on the coffee table in her haste but was skillfully able to dodge around it, saving herself a large bruise or scrape. Her heart pounded from the near miss and as she reached the window, she placed a hand over it. The other she planted flat against the glass. Outside a calm breeze gently rocked the tree tops. The streets were dry, all but around the curb. Wispy clouds drifted across the blue dome above giving the scene a tranquil aura. Across the road one man casually strolled. His grey felt jacket matched his ragged cowboy hat and chest length beard. He turned to her and smiled. Something about him was oddly familiar, though she couldn't place where she'd seen him before. His gentle eyes, heavy with crows feet brought out a calm, peaceful sensation which tingled through her weary body. She watched him go until he rounded the bend and vanished from view. With a sigh she turned away. The tear Donald shed glistened as though giving off its own pearl white glow. Carefully she picked it off the table and placed it on her open hand. It was her keepsake, a souvenir to remind her of the best thing to ever happen to her. A single tear trickled down her cheek. It fell to her palm and mingled with his. A warm sensation crept through her hand to her wrist. Through her entire body it swept, releasing with it a cascade of memories. Some were her own but most were Donald's. In that still moment she had lived his entire life, including not only the abuse, but the awesome energy the power had given. When the surge receded and the memories dwindled, she glanced to her palm once again. The tear drop was gone. In its place, glimmering residue left its mark. Fearing her trophy had fallen to the floor, she dropped to her knees and began a frantic search. It was nowhere to be seen. 'Why are you searching out here for me?' A faint inner voice whispered. She paused. 'You know where I am.' Again she looked at her hand. A shiver rippled up her spine and she came to realize the foreign substance had liquefied and absorbed into her flesh. What had been Donald's curse and blessing was now a part of her. "Oh my . . ." she breathed. There was no fear, no discouraging thoughts. This was a gift, Donald's final effort to keep them together. Their memories would forever intertwine until they again met. Maybe in this world, maybe the next. Who could say? "Goodbye for now, Donald." She murmured. "I'll never forget you."

Outside the old shack, the man dressed in grey wandered. The entrance to his underground home lay under the access cover of the sewer pipe out front. Lost in thought, he stared long and hard at the yellow tape across the front door. No one would be moving in any time soon, not that it mattered. It served its purpose for the time being. What troubled him was how to repair the damage done. Not the cracked interior walls or stained and rotting carpet, nor the dripping taps and cracks in the window frames which let in the cold weather. No, the problems he had to fix were much greater, beginning with Donald. From the roof he had gotten to know him. He was the best choice of all the children in the area. With nothing to lose he was primed to accept the telepathic gift, and it was freely given with the hope of setting him free of his abuser. Unfortunately for the boy's father, the plan had somewhat backfired. He wasn't supposed to die, but instead learn a valuable lesson and leave his son. Donald's new ability was to be his guardian. Had he only known the consequences, thing would've been different and his life could've gone on. It should've been made clear what was expected of him. Regardless, what was done was done. The boy would be no trouble to anyone in the future. His home in the underground burrow would keep him safe and others safe from him. He had failed the test. Was there anyone on the planet worthy of such a gift? Perhaps he hadn't been the ultimate test subject after all, despite doing well by standing up to his father regardless of the outcome. It took great encouragement to bring him to action back then, but when he finally dropped his passiveness and stood up for himself, he'd shown much promise. Unfortunately what lay unforeseen was how it went to his head as in most people. Give a little supremacy and watch it corrupt, hence the trouble with human nature. So predictable they were. From the oldest to youngest the one common bond they shared was an unwarranted need for control and a great lack of self restraint. Their race had much to learn. He popped the drain cover and climbed down iron rungs into the sewer. At the bottom behind a concrete wall, lay the oval ship he'd come to Earth in so long ago. Down here he could shed his disguise and reclaim his true form and with a snap decision he did. His once human flesh dissolved, leaving the shinny grey of his exterior skeleton glimmering in the dim light. He placed a hand on the wall which opened to his ship. If any human were to come down they would see a hologram of impenetrable concrete, not the elliptical alloy of an indestructible flying fortress. He checked his appearance in the reflection of the glossy metal. Compared to the human body, his was frail, bearing scrawny bony limbs, much longer than his counterpart. His head as well was elongated with no more than a lipless slit for a mouth. He had no ears to speak of. They weren't needed, for telepathy and vibrations guided him in a similar way. His nose, no more than a series of tiny holes, contained much more sensory glands, making his sense of smell more comparable to that of a dog. Had he been in human form his vision would be somewhat impaired, but as it was, even the night shone acutely. Human eyes were impressive with their unique colouring, unlike the bleakness of his own. Eagles and owls were two birds of prey to be greatly admired. Their sight matched his in almost every way, minus the ability to change their rainbow spectrum to any colour of choosing. It is what gave Donald the unorthodox hues in his fantasy worlds. Unfortunately it would be some time before those worlds could be cleansed from his imagination. Until he could remove all of the crystalline particles from his blood stream, they'd continue to both please and plague him and he would remain under the tempered carbon dome. Not the existence pre planned but until the process was complete, the one he was stuck with. It wasn't meant to be this way. He needed only to be kind and respect all creatures. The kitten had been the first test. He wouldn't hold it and had no desire to find it a home. Sherry Coleton would've allowed a pet, but no. Donald had to be the center of attention and spurn anything that threatened to take it from him. Out of spite he sent it away. The ducks were the second test which he failed equally fast. His attempt to harm them by kicking at them was not the final straw. It was sending Henry away blind that had done him in. It wasn't his fault he'd steadily grown irate to the point of violence. A side effect is all it was, brought on by Donald's dislike of male role models. It was unavoidable, which was why the decision to end the experiment came to pass. How much farther would he have gone without intervention? In the end, no one was safe. Not Sherry Coleton or Fiona Hemmingway, nor anyone whose paths crossed his. Jaden and William were at rest in similar confines, motionless in their glass encasements and surrounded by the array of multi-colored lights. When things were set right and the timeline restored, they'd be returned to their normal lives, unaware of their misfortune. Jaden's domineering attitude would be no more and William would no longer be the shy one, but assertive and strong. He'd be a help around the house, keeping up with his chores and attending family vacations with mom and new dad. It would be interesting to see how Sherry dealt with the telepathy crystals in **her** bloodstream. She was a wise woman and should be alright, though it would take time to perfect her new abilities. For the moment there was no need to put her through the purging process. For the sake of the family, Henry would not return. He would of course be healed and left to do what he did best, which was work. William would become the man he was destined to be and one day introduce a new species to the world. His kind would no longer hide among them, but live in harmony together. Two exceptional races no longer existing apart, but living as one. The outer door liquefied with his touch and he stepped through. Before it could solidify he took a long look down the dingy cavern. His home for now, but one day it would be above ground with his own kind. One day . . .

CPSIA information can be obtained at www.ICGtesting.com
Printed in the USA
244581LV00001B/21/P